Jacqueline pushed up from the table and came around to Raymond's side.

She put her arm around his waist and rested her head on his shoulder. "You're going to have a wonderful time, do all those things that families do when they get together and then you'll fly back."

Raymond turned on the stool and pulled her between his thighs. He looked up at her and caressed the side of her face with his finger. She lowered herself onto his lap. He tilted her chin upward and kissed her softly.

Jacqueline lightly draped her wrists on either side of his neck and looked into his eyes, seeing the history of their journey there, a journey that she was going to have to end. Her insides tightened.

When had their relationship gone from professional to personal? For several years it had been only business between them. It was the way it should have stayed but she'd made the mistake of letting Raymond slip past her defenses.

Books by Donna Hill

Harlequin Kimani Romance

Love Becomes Her
If I Were Your Woman
After Dark
Sex and Lies
Seduction and Lies
Temptation and Lies
Longing and Lies
Private Lessons
Spend My Life with You
Secret Attraction
Sultry Nights
Everything Is You

DONNA HILL

began writing novels in 1990. Since then she has had more than forty titles published, including full-length novels and novellas. Two of her novels and one novella were adapted for television. She has won numerous awards for her body of work. She is also the editor of five novels, two of which were nominated for awards. She easily moves from romance to erotica, horror, comedy and women's fiction. She was the first recipient of an *RT Book Reviews* Trailblazer Award, won an *RT Book Reviews* Career Achievement Award and currently teaches writing at the Frederick Douglass Creative Arts Center.

Donna lives in Brooklyn with her family. Visit her website at www.donnahill.com.

EVERYTHING IS *You*

DONNA HILL

HARLEQUIN®
entertain, enrich, inspire™

Recycling programs
for this product may
not exist in your area.

ISBN-13: 978-0-373-86284-9

EVERYTHING IS YOU

Copyright © 2012 by Donna Hill

www.Harlequin.com

Printed in U.S.A.

Dear Reader

Thank you for selecting *Everything Is You*. If you are new to the series, welcome to the intriguing world of the Lawsons of Louisiana! You are in for a treat. This time, I want to introduce you to Jacqueline Lawson, the younger sister of patriarch Sr. Senator Branford Lawson. Jacqueline has been estranged from her family for years, for a variety of reasons. She has not spoken with her brother for nearly a decade. But she's made a life for herself as an award-winning, international photojournalist. Enter Raymond Jordan, a celebrated journalist in his own right. The two travel the world together. Raymond wants more but Jacqueline knows that she can never commit and the only person who may be able to change that is her brother Branford.

Everything Is You is a tribute to a man whose love for a woman will stop at nothing and who will move mountains to have her. It is about an independent woman who finds that she does need something and someone more. It is about a powerful family, rife with drama, secrets, sexy men and dynamic women. Welcome!

Be sure to follow the entire series: *Spend My Life with You*, *Secret Attraction*, *Sultry Nights* and now *Everything Is You*. You will also find many of the Lawson clan in my new series Sag Harbor Village, beginning with *Touch Me Now*.

Until next time,

Donna

Chapter 1

A yellow cab turned onto South Figueroa and eased to a stop in front of The Beacon Hill Towers. Jacqueline Lawson stepped out into the late, balmy Los Angeles afternoon. The red-vested doorman pulled open the glass-and-chrome door of the condominium as she approached.

"Afternoon, Ms. Lawson."

Jacqueline smiled but it didn't reach her eyes that remained hidden behind wide, dark shades. Her maple-brown skin glistened in the June sun. "Hi, Bobby. Hot out here today." She lifted the weight of her ponytail from her neck to catch some air.

"Yes, ma'am. They say thunderstorms."

"How's your wife and daughter?" she asked, stepping into the cool embrace of the lobby.

"They're well. Thanks. There's a package for you at the front desk."

"Thanks, Bobby." She adjusted her tote bag over her shoulder. Her teal-colored sling-back heels tapped out a slow but steady rhythm against the terra cotta floor. She approached the concierge desk. "Hi, Mike. Bobby said I have a package."

"Sure do. Would you like me to send it up? It's kind of heavy."

"Yes, please. Send it up later. Thanks." She started off toward the elevator and the room swayed. She slowed her step and drew in a steadying breath. The warning words of her doctor echoed in her head. Concentrating, she walked to the bank of elevators. Exhaustion rode through her in waves. She squeezed her eyes closed for a moment and willed herself to remain upright.

The elevator dinged and the polished stainless steel doors silently slid open. A young, very tanned couple exited, gave brief nods and moved past her.

Jacqueline stepped inside, thankful to be alone as the doors closed behind her. She leaned against the back wall for support. She was running out of time and her options were limited.

The doors slid open on the eighteenth floor and Jacqueline pushed herself forward down the hallway that was decorated with fresh flowers on antique tabletops and black-and-white art on the walls. Her two-bedroom apartment was at the end of the hall that she shared with one other tenant.

Once inside she adjusted the cooling system and walked into her bedroom that opened onto a panoramic view of Downtown Los Angeles.

Item by item she stripped out of her clothes and tossed them into a hamper in the bathroom. She took her silk robe from a hook on the back of the door and slid it on, tying the belt loosely around her waist.

She needed to lie down. The simple trip to the doctor's office had drained her more than she'd anticipated. She stretched out on the bed and then turned onto her side curling into a half fetal position.

That's the way Raymond found her when he came in an hour later, carrying the box that had been delivered earlier.

He placed the box in the corner near the chaise lounge and quietly approached. He leaned down and placed a feathery light kiss on her forehead. She stirred ever so slightly, murmuring something that he could not make out. He eased out of the room and shut the bedroom door halfway, deciding to surprise her with an early dinner. He took a quick shower, changed into his favorite weatherworn navy blue sweatpants and padded barefoot into the living space that opened onto the kitchen. He crossed the shining hardwood floor to the entertainment unit. The gleam of Jacqueline's Associated Press Medal for photojournalism sat in its place of honor encased in glass. Every time he looked at it a feeling of pride puffed his chest, reminding him of what an incredible woman she was and the fearlessness that it took for her to earn it. He turned on the stereo to his favorite R&B station.

Since their return from their last assignment in the rain forests of the Amazon, Jacqueline had been quiet and withdrawn. Initially, he thought she was worn out from the grueling three months of the trip or that she'd caught a bug. But she insisted that she was fine.

Raymond pulled open the double door stainless steel refrigerator and opened the vegetable bin drawer. He took out fresh spinach, baby tomatoes, a box of mushrooms and a cucumber and prepared a quick side salad. Jacqueline loved pasta and it was the one thing he was good at in the kitchen. He washed and deveined a half pound of shrimp and then sautéed fresh garlic in a light olive oil. He tossed the cleaned shrimp into the sizzling pan, while the water boiled for the pasta.

"Hey."

Raymond turned from the sink. He smiled at her still sleepy-eyed appearance. "Hey, yourself. Get enough rest?"

She nodded her head, covered her yawn and tightened the belt on her robe. "What are you doing?"

"Fixing dinner. Figured you'd be hungry. I know I am." He plucked a shrimp from the pan and walked over to her. He held it tauntingly above her lips. She opened her mouth and he dropped it in.

She chewed slowly. "Hmmm."

He grinned. "It'll be ready soon."

She sat down on the counter stool. "How long have you been here?"

"'Bout an hour or so." He dropped the pasta into the boiling water and then opened the refrigerator and took out a bottle of beer. "Want one?" he asked holding up a bottle of Rochefort Trappistes *10*.

Jacqueline propped her chin up on her hands. "A new one?"

"Yeah, and you'll love it. It's a Belgium brew." His smooth brows bounced.

Besides being an award-winning photographer, Raymond was a beer connoisseur and collector. His house in the valley had a room with some of the most rare and expensive beers in the world. He'd been featured in *All About Beer* and *Beer Connoisseur* magazines on several occasions. And whatever part of the world that they traveled he always had to try out the beer.

He opened a bottle and handed it to her. He watched her in anticipation while she took her first sip. Her hazel eyes shifted to a warm brown and her lids fluttered closed as she savored the dark color, full-bodied taste with hints of strong plum, raisin and black currant.

"Hmmm," she hummed in appreciation, rolling the liquid around on her tongue. She'd always been a white wine and martini girl, but Raymond had expanded her taste buds. In her head she equated beer to guys sharing a six-pack while watching baseball and eating hot dogs. He turned beer drinking into an exotic experience.

Raymond clapped his hands. "Great. I knew you'd love it." He turned back to the stove, took the pasta off the flame and drained it in the sink. He mixed chopped baby tomatoes, fresh basil, olive oil and ground black pepper, and tossed it with the pasta in a large serving plate. He took the cooked shrimp from the skillet, layered them on top then sprinkled the dish with fresh Parmesan cheese.

Jacqueline got up and took two plates down from the cabinet over the sink. Raymond seized the opportunity of her close proximity to slide his arm around her waist and planted a kiss behind her ear. She moved easily away.

"I'm actually starved," she said, not looking at him while she put the plates on the counter.

Raymond watched the way she kept her back to him, the calculated way that she placed each item next to the other.

"So...what did you do today?" he asked, giving the pasta one last toss.

For a moment she stilled. "Met Traci for brunch," she said a bit too cheery. "She asked about you." She looked at him quickly before turning away.

Raymond brought the plate to the counter along with the serving tongs. "Salad is in the fridge."

"I'll get it."

They sat down opposite each other and dished out the pasta.

"Looks and smells delicious," Jacqueline said, staying focused on her plate.

Raymond studied her from beneath his lashes. "When are you going to tell me what's going on with you?"

"What do you mean?"

"You know what I mean, Jacquie. You're tired all the time, you barely want me to touch you, you won't hold a real conversation… Do I need to go on? You haven't been the same since we got back."

She blinked rapidly, reached for her bottle of beer but put it down. "Ray…" She pushed out a breath.

"Say it. Say what you've been trying *not* to say for weeks."

She looked at him, stared deep into his eyes and saw her own hurt and confusion swimming in the dark depths.

"I'm tired. Plain and simple. Can't I be tired? I'm not superwoman, you know. I've been working nonstop for the past year in every nook and cranny on the planet," she said, throwing her hand up in the air. "And the last thing I need is you bugging me to death about it." She took a long swallow of beer and set it down then ran her hand through the spiral twists of her hair. She turned her head away. "I'm sorry." She looked at him. "Can we enjoy this nice meal that you toiled over and talk about something else?" She offered a strained smile. "Please."

Raymond exhaled a long frustrated breath. "You're a difficult woman, J," he conceded. "I'm gonna let it go for now."

"Good." She turned her attention to her pasta. "You want me to drive you to the airport in the morning?"

He cocked a brow. "You want to?"

"Of course."

"Thanks. By the way, the invitation for my parents' fiftieth anniversary party arrived yesterday. The celebration takes place in three months, and I wish you would come with me."

She kept her eyes on her plate. "I told you, I don't do family."

"You never talk about your family."

"Nothing to talk about." She stirred her food around in her plate.

"Another non-topic," he murmured.

Jacqueline chose to ignore the barb. She'd put physical miles and emotional distance between her and her family for years. She periodically stayed in touch with her nieces, LeAnn, Dominique and Desiree, and nephews Rafe and Justin. But she hadn't spoken to her brother in years. She was not of the mighty Lawson ilk. She made her own name and her own way in the world. She refused to be dictated to by her brother the way he did everyone else. The people in her life didn't even know that she was related to the royal Lawson clan of Louisiana. And that's the way she wanted to keep it, including Raymond.

Raymond studied her while he finished off his beer. What happened between her and her brother? She never talked about Branford Lawson and had he not done some digging on his own he would have never known that they were related. Crazy. But he would respect her wishes, even if he didn't understand her reasons. To him, family was sacred. He came from a large, loving, all-in-your-business family. He couldn't imagine not having them in his life. But Jacqueline Lawson was a complex woman. It was what he loved about her, but he'd kept that to himself as well.

Jacqueline pushed up from the table and came around to Raymond's side. She put her arm around his waist and rested her head on his shoulder. "You're going to have a wonderful time, do all those things that families do when they get together and then you'll fly back."

Raymond turned on the stool and pulled her between his thighs. He looked up at her and caressed the side of her face with his finger. She lowered herself onto his lap. He tilted her chin upward and kissed her softly.

Jacqueline lightly draped her delicate wrists on either side of his neck and looked into his dark almost black eyes, seeing the history of their journey there, a journey that she was going to have to end. Her insides tightened.

When had their relationship gone from professional to personal? For several years it had been only business between them. It was the way it should have stayed but she'd made the mistake of letting Raymond slip past her defenses.

They'd met quite by accident at the National Association of Black Journalists a few years ago, at the annual awards dinner in Washington, D.C....

Chapter 2

Jacqueline never enjoyed those stuffed shirt affairs. She'd sweltered in them most of her young life growing up in the Lawson household where the sun shining was reason enough to throw a gala. Her mother and father—God rest their souls—were Southern royalty. Her father's closest friends were those that most people only read about. And her mother was in her glory entertaining them. The Lawson home was and remained the central hub for the comings and goings of the political, corporate and entertainment Who's Who. And her brothers Branford and David were cut from the same cloth.

Perhaps it was because she was the youngest—a change of life baby, as her mother always reminded her—and a girl, that her father focused all of his attention on her brothers and her mother turned her over to the nanny so that she could conduct her charity events and social climbing.

Jacqueline never felt part of the family but more of an afterthought. So she made her own way, built her own life and over time the tenuous ties that bound her to her family were severed. The final cut being her brother David.

Unfortunately, those once per year events were part and parcel of her business and as reluctant as she was to admit it, she did learn from living it, that rubbing elbows was needed and necessary. And, besides, it was one of the few times that she did have a chance to interact with her colleagues and see some of the important work they were doing and being recognized for.

When she'd walked into the grand ballroom at the Kennedy Center she immediately wished that she'd brought a date. She pasted on her best smile and wandered over to the bar. The crutch of a glass of white wine could hold her up for at least an hour if she sipped really slowly. And if she found a comfortable leaning position or a good seat out of the way, her feet encased in "sex me" heels would last through the long evening.

"You look like you hate this almost as much as I do."

She angled her head to the right and inhaled a short, sharp breath. *Yummy* was her first thought before she could respond.

"Is it that obvious?" She arched a questioning brow

as her photographic eye took him in from head to toe in one click of her internal lens.

The amazing dark chocolate-brown eyes twinkled in the light and creased at the edges when he smiled down at her. She wasn't a big gospel fan but he sure could be a body double for the singer BeBe Winans with the dulcet tone to go with the look. And that body appeared totally comfortable and sleek in his tux.

"You have the ever ready wineglass. The casual lean against the bar pose…" His gaze traveled down. "…to keep the pressure off of those pretty feet."

She bit back a smile.

"And the…'just how long is this thing gonna last,' look in your eyes." He turned to the bar and picked up his glass of Hennessey on the rocks then returned his attention back to her.

"Observant."

"Occupational hazard. Journalist?"

"Photographic."

He nodded slowly in appreciation.

"You?"

"Foreign correspondent."

She switched her wine flute from her right hand to her left and extended her hand. "Jacqueline."

"Raymond Jordan." His hand enveloped hers.

He smelled good, too. "Nice to meet you."

"You have a table?"

"No. Do you?"

"Naw." He took a swallow of his drink. "I figured

there had to be an available seat in here somewhere. After all, I pay my dues and I did get an invite."

She giggled. "My sentiments exactly."

"Care to spend the evening with another jaded guest?"

Jacqueline glanced up at him. "Sure, why not."

Raymond crooked his elbow and Jacqueline hooked her arm through.

They found a table in the center of the room with two empty seats at a table for eight. After a bit of seat shifting they settled next to each other and were soon served appetizers for the sit-down dinner.

Up front, CNN correspondent Anderson Cooper was in conversation with Karen Ballard, who specialized in motion picture photography. Jacqueline and Raymond whispered conspiratorially about Cooper's possible appearance in a film and they entertained themselves by concocting stories about the plethora of attendees that spanned the gamut of journalism, and swapped stories about some of their memorable assignments.

Raymond was equally as traveled as Jacqueline and spoke three languages fluently, compared to her two. He'd lived in Japan for a year, spent several summers in Europe and loved motorcycle riding.

"What was it like being embedded with the troops in Iraq?" he asked.

"Scary. But I knew that they wouldn't let anything happen to me. I was there to do a job and they respected that." She glanced off.

"Must have been tough. The things you saw…"

She nodded. "It was." She turned and looked into his eyes. "The sad part is, I've seen and photographed worse."

"I know. In this business when you think you've seen everything there's one more thing that sucks the air out of your lungs."

"Fortunately, there's still some beauty left in the world."

"Fortunately," he said and raised his glass to her, his gaze moving with appreciation across her face.

After a long line of award-winners and acceptance speeches, the event wound down to a glittering close.

Jacqueline and Raymond made their way out through the throng of bodies.

"Going to the after party?" Raymond asked once they were outside.

"Oh no," she said, waving her hand. "I've had enough party people to last me at least until this time next year."

Raymond chuckled. "Live here or staying in town?"

"Actually, I'm only here until tomorrow. I fly out in the morning. Off to Israel for the next month."

"Busy lady. Where do you call home?"

She hesitated for a moment. Louisiana was where she was born but it hadn't been home for a very long time. "California."

His head jerked back in surprise. "Me too."

"That's just a pickup line, right?"

"No." He chuckled. "Seriously. I moved out there

about a year ago from Maplewood, New Jersey. I'm in San Fernando Valley. Been there about two years now."

"Hmmm. Small world."

"Maybe we can get together the next time we're in the same time zone."

Jacqueline offered a half smile. She lifted her arm to signal for the next taxi in line.

A cab pulled up in front of them. Raymond stepped forward and opened the door for her. She ducked in the cab.

Raymond stuck his head in. "Safe travels, pretty lady. Thanks for spending the evening with me."

There was no room in her life for a man like Raymond, for any man or anyone. She didn't stay put long enough for a relationship to have any meaning. And there was no point in opening the door to something that would never get a chance to cross the threshold.

"Take care," she said and for a brief instant, she wished things could be different, but they weren't.

Raymond gave her a wistful parting smile, shut the door and stepped back.

She watched him in the rearview mirror until the cab turned the corner. She was sure that was the last time she would see him and in the ensuing months she often wondered what part of the world he was in. Sometimes she would run across his byline only to realize that he was a half a world away.

And then one day, there he was in the Khan el-

Khalili market in Cairo, thousands of miles away from where they'd met nearly a year earlier.

"Ray?" She approached from his right. He turned and swiped his dark shades from his eyes. His grin spread like the sun rising over the ocean and moved through her.

"Jacquie, what in the world…"

She giggled like a schoolgirl. "You stole my line."

He tossed his head back and laughed from deep in his belly. "This is one of those crazy surprises…a good one," he added. He put down the bolt of white cotton that he'd been considering purchasing. "You look…different." He'd memorized her in the clinging off-white cocktail dress that flirted with her knees and showed off incredible legs. The diamonds at her throat and wrist, the way the dip of the dress teased the senses with hints of what lay beneath. Her scent that he couldn't get out of his head…and those eyes. Those eyes. And that lush full mouth. And now she looked like a gorgeous cover-model for college girls with her hair pulled back into a ponytail, a khaki baseball cap, T-shirt that barely contained those lush breasts and khaki shorts. Totally delicious.

"Must be the sneakers," she teased.

He snapped his fingers. "That's it!" He stepped closer. "How long are you here for?"

"At least another two weeks. You?"

"Me too. I'm on assignment to cover the Summit."

"So am I," she said, inexplicably happy.

"Have any free time on your schedule? Maybe we can have dinner or do the tourist thing."

"Yeah." She nodded. "I'd like that."

"Where are you staying?"

"The Semiramis Intercontinental."

"I'm at the Atlas Zamalek. Are you free later tonight?"

"I have to caption some photos, but that should only take a few hours. How about eight?"

"No problem. I'll come by your hotel."

She bobbed her head. "Okay. I'll meet you in the lobby." She took a step back. "I, uh, have some errands to run so…I'll see you at eight."

"Eight."

She turned to leave.

"Hey, Jacquie."

She looked back over her shoulder. "You never told me your last name."

"Lawson."

Chapter 3

"Hey," Raymond said softly, moving his head back and forth in front of her.

Jacqueline blinked away the past and Ray came back into focus. She forced a smile.

"Where did you just go?"

She blew out a breath and shook her shoulders a bit. "I just realized that I didn't get to open my package." She took his hand and pulled him to his feet. "Come, I want to show you."

"Is it more equipment, J?" How many times had he watched her face light up when she discovered a new use for a lens or composed a picture a different way or purchased the latest waterproof camera? And how many times had he wished that he'd see the same kind of excitement in her eyes for him? It came only in flashes, nothing ever sustained. And when it did, she would shut it down, turn off the lights as if she was afraid he would see whatever it was that she was trying to hide.

"Hush, and just come on."

They trooped into her bedroom and she went over to the box that Raymond had placed in the corner.

She duckwalked it over to the side table near the bed. "It *isn't* heavy, just awkward." Her long slender fingers quickly stripped the box of the securing tape and pulled open the flaps.

Reverently she reached inside and took out the first box that contained the jaw-dropping Canon EOS 5D Mark III. Gently she removed it from its packaging and placed it on the table. The second box contained the equally spectacular new Nikon D800. Even Raymond had to admit he was impressed. These were top-of-the-line cameras and together cost more than six thousand dollars.

The remaining contents were a camera bag, lenses and memory cards. Where many women splurged on clothes and shoes, Jacqueline poured her extra cash on photographic equipment. She said it was an investment in her business. And she was right. Her equipment alone was worth millions and she had the perfect piece ready for any assignment. Not only did she purchase the latest in photographic equipment, she was a collector of antique cameras as well. She had one room of her three-bedroom condo dedicated to her equipment.

"Impressive," Raymond murmured in appreciation. He picked up the Nikon and held it up to his face, adjusting the lens to take in the room. The powerful lens brought the skyline of Los Angeles into sharp relief.

"Nice," he said, drawing out the word. "Very nice." He gingerly put the camera down and turned to Jacqueline, who was examining the Canon.

She glanced up at him. There was that smile, but he knew it wasn't for him but for her toys.

"At some point you are going to run out of space," he teased.

"Yeah, I've been thinking the same thing." She shrugged off the prospect. Running out of space would mean either giving up some of her toys or moving. She didn't relish either idea. She'd been approached on several occasions to donate some of her antique cameras to museums. That was always an option.

A shadow slowly crept over the room as if the lights were dimmed, followed by a bright flash of light just above the skyline. Jacqueline gasped at the boom that sounded like the bombs they'd both heard and lived through in war torn countries.

She momentarily shut her eyes against the frightening noise. Raymond hurried over to the French doors that were blown open onto the terrace. He fought against the wind and lashing rain that ferociously beat down everything in its path, to get the doors closed.

He managed to pull the doors shut but not without a cost. He turned slowly around.

Jacqueline hid her giggle behind her hand. Just that quickly he was drenched from head to foot.

"Let me get you a towel." She scampered off to the linen closet and brought back a towel, to find Raymond pulling his T-shirt over his head and stepping out of his damp sweatpants.

There was nothing to say about Ray's physique other than perfection. He was toned from his workouts but also from the hard and fast life that he lived. Traversing mountains, slicing his way through tropical jungles, treading across rushing rivers were all as common to him as another man who went to the office in a suit and tie.

She wished that she could say that was the only attraction, that it was only physical. It wasn't. That's what made this all so painfully hard. Would she ever stop wanting him, needing him? Her chest tightened while a flash of how empty her life would be without Raymond in it ran through her.

She walked up to him and tenderly stroked his face with the towel, then across his broad shoulders and down his bare chest.

Raymond clasped her by the wrists and pulled her flush against him.

"When am I ever going to stop wanting you," he growled deep in his throat. He cupped her face in his hands and swept down to kiss her. A hungry longing roared through him the way it always did when he touched her.

Jacqueline moaned against his mouth. Her body instantly responded to the fire that he lit in her belly. She moved closer, parted her lips to let him in. She wrapped her arms around him, giving in to her need this one last time. Her heart thundered as the rain pounded against the windows.

Raymond lifted her off her feet and walked with her to her bed.

It was all so familiar yet different every time that he touched her, made her body come alive in new ways. Her skin sang beneath his fingertips and her insides vibrated with desire. His mouth was hot and wet and everywhere that it touched it set her ablaze.

When he entered her, the world came apart in a million little pieces. And with each thrust, every kiss, touch and moan the pieces came together and exploded again and again.

The sky lit up beyond them and her body swirled around him like the wicked wind and his love poured into her like the falling rain.

Jacqueline fought back her tears and held him to her, listening to the familiar beat of his heart, knowing that this was the last time.

Chapter 4

Raymond slung his carry-on over his shoulder as he stepped out of Jacqueline's midnight blue Mercedes sports coup. She popped the trunk and he came around to the back of the car and took out his bag and laptop. Jacqueline met him on the curb. Frenzied travelers swirled around them. Traffic cops and security personnel waved cars along the busy drop off lane and warned the drivers of parked vehicles to move it along. She looked up at him, hooking her thumbs into the loops of his jeans.

"Try to stay out of trouble while I'm gone," he said with a catch in his throat. He gave her a lopsided grin.

"What fun would that be?" she teased.

He slowly lowered his head, and brushed his lips against hers.

Jacqueline's heart thundered and guilt welled up in her throat. She longed to tell him but she couldn't do that to him. It was best this way. Her eyes burned. She blinked away the threat of tears.

Raymond stepped back and tenderly stroked her cheek. "See you in a week. What should I bring you from Indonesia?"

"Surprise me," she managed over the knot in her throat. She wiped away the gloss of her lipstick from his lips with the pad of her thumb. "You're going to miss your flight."

He kissed her one last time before grabbing the bag. He turned toward the revolving doors.

"Ray…"

He turned. *Tell him,* her conscience whispered. The words stuck in her throat. "Have a safe trip," she uttered instead.

His smile made his eyes crinkle in the corners. "I will." And then he was gone, swallowed up in the mass of humanity.

Jacqueline stood there until a security officer told her to move or get her car towed. With a heavy heart she rounded the front of her car, slid behind the wheel and pulled off.

Jacqueline took a sip of her apple martini. The bar was crowded, but that was to be expected on a Thursday night. The live band had begun their first set when Traci walked in. She stood and waved above heads and shoulders to get Traci's attention.

Traci Desmond was an independent documentary filmmaker. They'd met more than fifteen years ago when they were students at New York University. They had the same media arts class and they hit it off from day one. They'd been friends ever since. Traci was the sister she never had and the only person she trusted enough with her darkest secrets. Traci had been there for Jacqueline through it all, as Jacqueline was for her.

"Hey, girl." Traci kissed Jacqueline's cheek and slid onto the seat opposite her. "Busy night, I see." She placed her purse on her lap. "Ray get off okay?"

Jacqueline nodded and took a sip from her drink.

"You still didn't tell him you were going to your niece's wedding, I take it? Or anything else of importance."

"No."

Traci blew out a breath of frustration. "J, I love you. You know that, but I swear I do not understand why you won't tell him."

Jacqueline stared at her friend over the rim of her glass. "Yes, you do," she said in a monotone.

Traci pursed her full lips. "But I don't have to like it."

"It's better this way."

"Secrets, lies? You call that better?"

"I don't need a lecture, Traci. Seriously."

"Fine," she said in a feigned huff. "What time is your flight to Louisiana?"

"Tomorrow afternoon at two."

A waitress stopped at the table and took Traci's drink order.

"How do you think it will go?"

She shrugged her right shoulder. "I don't know," she said on a breath. "I haven't spoken to my brother in ten years. I haven't seen my nieces and nephews in almost as long. I missed Lee Ann's wedding." She slowly turned her glass around on the table. "I was in the Sudan or somewhere. I don't even remember. But I don't want to miss Desi's. Who knows when…if I'll get to see any of them again."

Traci studied her for a moment. "Are you going to tell Branford what's going on?"

She shook her head. "No."

Traci clasped her hands together on top of the table. "He's your brother, J. Your flesh and blood. And I'm going to be honest with you, because I'm your friend and I know you. You talk a good talk about not needing anyone, not needing your family and wanting to make your own way. But you do care and if you gave them half a chance I know that they care about you, too." She tipped her head to the side and looked at Jacqueline through lowered lids. "If you really didn't want to see them—and maybe even talk to your brother—you could have simply sent a gift." She cocked an eyebrow to emphasize her point.

Jacqueline's eyes flashed for a moment. She lowered her gaze and stared down into her glass.

"You're going to have to stop traveling soon. You may not be able to work. What are you going to do then if you shut everyone out—especially Raymond?"

Jacqueline tossed back the rest of her drink. "Let's order. I'm starved." She set down her glass and then snapped open the menu.

Traci knew that look. The walls were up and there wasn't anything that she would be able to do to get Jacqueline to talk short of bamboo shoots under her nails. Every fiber of her being wanted to shake some sense into Jacqueline, but knowing Jacquie, she'd cuss her out and make her pay for dinner. She may not be able to fix things between Jacquie and her family or her and Raymond. What she could do was be her friend.

"I think I'll have the steak," Traci said. "With sweet potato fries. They are the best this side of anywhere."

Jacqueline smiled. "Yeah, that sounds good."

Traci stared at her from across the table. "How are you feeling?"

She gave a slight shrug. "The same. Tired. Had a little dizzy spell yesterday, but I think it was from the heat."

"What did the doctor say?"

Jacqueline blew out a breath. "The readings are the same. At least I'm no worse."

"Hmm."

The waitress returned and took their dinner orders and Traci's request for a mango daiquiri.

"I need you to promise me something."

"Sure."

"No matter what happens do not say anything to Raymond. You have to promise me."

Traci swallowed. "J..."

"Promise me," she insisted.

"All right, all right. I promise."

Jacqueline released a breath of relief. "Thank you. And you'll oversee the movers, make sure that everything gets packed up?"

Traci blinked back tears. "Yes," she murmured. "J, you don't have to do this. You shouldn't do this."

"I'm not going to talk about it anymore. It's done. Okay."

They looked everywhere but each other in a strained silence.

"I can get off early and take you to the airport," Traci finally said.

She shook her head. "No. I'll be fine. I'll go to the wedding, make nice and then start my...new life."

Traci looked away for a moment. The enormity of what Jacqueline was planning to do had haunted her for months. She'd tried without success to talk Jacqueline out of this irrational upheaval of her life. But with each visit to the doctor, and medication that no longer worked, Jacqueline had made up her mind and was resolute that this was the only way. And Traci knew that

Jacqueline's will was a mighty force. If she could cut her family off, walk out on the one man in her life that had touched her soul, distance herself from her best friend, she was a woman whose determination and focus could not be shaken with pleas.

"What did you get Desiree for her wedding gift?"

"A cut crystal bowl from Tiffany. Not anything that you can use very often but it looks pretty." She grinned. "I had it shipped to my hotel. Hopefully it arrived in one piece."

"Anything would be better than shipping it on a passenger plane."

"How 'bout that." She gazed off. "It'll be good to see everyone," she said wistfully.

"I know they'll be glad to see you."

The waitress returned with Traci's drink. She lifted it toward Jacqueline. "To a safe trip and a happy reunion."

Jacqueline slowly lifted her glass and gently touched it to Traci's. "To promises," she said and took a sip.

The cab made the turn onto France Street and pulled up in front of The Belle of Baton Rouge. The driver climbed out to help Jacqueline with her bags just as a bellhop approached with a luggage cart.

"Welcome to The Belle," he greeted and took the two Louis Vuitton suitcases from the driver and placed them on the cart.

Jacqueline paid the driver and included a generous tip. They'd battled airport traffic for more than an hour for a ride that should have taken half that time. But all during the trip the driver regaled her with lively stories of his family that included six children under the age of fifteen and a wife who, according to him, was a saint.

"Thank you so much. And happy anniversary."

He grinned broadly, his nut-brown face glistening from the humidity. "Thank you," he said with a slight bow of his bald head. "I hope you enjoy your stay."

"So do I." She followed the bellhop into the cool interior of the lobby. The heat and humidity were two things that she definitely did not miss about her hometown. She walked up to the check-in counter.

"Welcome to The Belle," the young blonde reservationist greeted. "Your name?"

"Jacqueline Lawson." She took off her wide shades and looked around at the plush lobby.

She clicked a few keys on the computer. "Yes, Ms. Lawson. We have you in the suite on the tenth floor for three nights. I will need your credit card for incidentals."

"Sure." She dug in her purse and took out her wallet, fished through her cards and handed over her American Express.

"How many keys will you be needing?"

"Just one, thanks."

She processed her room key and handed it to Jacqueline along with her credit card. "If you're ready, I can have someone take up your bags."

"Yes, please."

"John will help you with your bags. And you have a package. Would you like that brought up as well?"

"Thank you. Yes."

The bellhop came up to the desk.

"Tenth floor," the receptionist said. "Enjoy your stay."

"Right this way, ma'am."

"First time to Baton Rouge?" the young man asked once they were aboard the elevator.

"No. But it's my first time back in a number of years."

"Are you here for the wedding? The city has been buzzing about it for weeks."

"Wedding?"

"Yes, one of Senator Lawson's daughters is getting married tomorrow. A real big event from what I'm hearing." He frowned a moment. "Are you related?"

Jacqueline quickly shook her head. "No. Just coincidence."

"My apologies. Same name and all."

"Hmm, I get that a lot," she murmured.

The bell tinged and the doors slid open giving her the perfect escape from his question. The least everyone knew about her the better. Coming back to her hometown was hard enough. She didn't want to make any unnecessary connection between herself and the fabled Lawson family.

John wheeled the cart down the carpeted hall to room 1012. Jacqueline used her key and opened the door to pure luxury. The room opened onto a sprawling living space, fully furnished with a sleek, copper-toned couch, matching love seat and chair and a footstool. Low, glass-and-wood tables held blooming flora in bursting colors of orange, teal blue and white. The back wall was a window of glass that looked out onto the sprawling city. A full service bar was to the right, and beyond was a kitchen fit for a chef.

"Should I put these in the bedroom?"

"Yes, please." She followed him down a short hall to the bedroom that was equally as lavish as the front. A king-size bed dominated the room, draped in all white. Dark cherry wood furnishings and a chaise lounge completed the room. A flat-screen television was mounted on the wall. French doors opened to a small terrace. It was well worth the money she spent.

John went to the closet and took out the luggage stand and placed the bags on top. "Enjoy your stay."

Jacqueline reached into her bag and took out her purse. She handed him a ten-dollar tip.

He beamed his gratitude. "Thank you," he said, bowing his way out of the door.

Jacqueline placed her purse on the small table near the terrace and opened the doors. She stepped outside and drew in a lungful of husky Louisiana air. Her gaze slowly took in the skyline.

Beyond the cityscape was the Lawson mansion, the place she'd once called home.

Chapter 5

Just as Jacqueline was getting settled, there was a knock at her door. She tied the belt around her robe and went to the door. The bellhop had her box.

"Your package, Ms. Lawson."

She reached for it.

"I can put it inside for you."

"Oh, of course." She stepped aside to let him pass. "You can put it right there on that table."

He soundlessly crossed the room and gingerly set the large box on the glass-and-wood table.

"Thank you," she said, walking him to the door. She grabbed her purse took out her wallet and pressed a five dollar bill into his hand.

"Enjoy your stay, Ms. Lawson," he said with a smile of appreciation.

This could get expensive. She closed the door behind him and walked over to where he'd left the box. She tore off the packing tape and tucked inside the foam balls and plastic was the iconic blue Tiffany box. Gingerly she untied the ribbon from around the box and lifted the cover. The stunning crystal bowl sparkled inside. She checked it for cracks and then closed the lid and retied the ribbon.

For a moment she paused with her hands on the box. The realization that she would see her family in less than twenty-four hours suddenly hit her. She *did* miss her nieces and nephews. It had been so long and the gap had only widened during the ensuing years of their estrangement. As for her brother, well that was a different story. She often wondered if he thought about her at all. And her nephew Maurice, David's son, no one, not even she had heard from him in ages. She worried about Maurice the most. He'd been devastated by his father's death. She had her reasons for turning away from her family but he did, as well.

A sudden wave of dizziness seized her and she gripped the edge of the table for support. She closed her eyes and breathed deeply. She could hear her pulse pounding in her ears. The room seemed to shift then slowly settled. Jacqueline opened her eyes. In an instant the rest of what her life would be like flashed through her head like a bad "B" movie. This visit to her family was as much an extension of the olive branch as it was a goodbye. She didn't want their pity, sympathy or help. But she did want to see them again, as she was now, not how she would eventually become.

Gathering her strength she went into her bedroom for a nap when her cell phone rang. She walked over to the nightstand and picked up the phone. Raymond's name was illuminated on the face of the phone.

She drew in a sobering breath and touched the talk icon. "Hi!" she said, forcing cheer into her voice. She sat down on the side of the bed.

"Hey, babe."

The timbre of his voice, as always, rolled through her in warm waves.

"How was your flight?"

"Long," he said with a chuckle. "But it's just a layover. The second leg of the flight is in another hour. Wish you were here."

"You'll be there and settled in no time," she said, sidestepping his comment.

"Yeah, as settled as I generally get on these things. The humidity here is stifling. I could take ten showers and it would never be enough. How about you? What were you doing? I was hoping I didn't wake you. This time difference always screws me up."

"Oh, nothing. Playing with my new toys," she said, the lies sliding across her tongue with ease.

He laughed. And she missed him. Her throat clenched. "So…what's on your agenda?"

"Day after tomorrow, I meet with the ambassador at the embassy. He's giving me an hour."

His trip to Indonesia was to investigate and write an extensive piece of the evolving strife within the government. There had been several uprising of opposing forces within the past six months that had the United States wary of a possible coup. This assignment had Pulitzer written all over it.

"I'm hoping to gain access to some of the members of the opposition. The story has to be balanced. And of course, traveling throughout Jakarta and some of the outlying areas to get some insight from the people."

"Just be careful, Ray," she said with more emotion than she intended.

"Of course." He paused. "Are you all right? You sound funny."

"No, no, I'm fine." She swallowed.

"I know you don't like it when I question you, but I've been worried about you, J. I hated to leave."

She lowered her head. She so wanted to tell him, to unburden her soul, pour out her fears and have him wrap his arms around her and tell her that he would make everything all right. But she would not condemn him to the life that was on the horizon for her. That's not what you did to someone that you loved.

"You worry entirely too much."

"I'm supposed to."

Her bottom lip trembled. She had to get off the phone

or she was certain she would break down. "I know you have to be exhausted."

He yawned as if on cue. "I am. Twenty-four hours flying across time zones are for men half my age," he joked.

Jacqueline laughed. "You love it. You always have. And you look kinda good for your age."

"Very funny. But," he yawned again, "if I don't get some sleep I'm going to feel like seventy-six instead of thirty-six."

"Then get some rest when you can. We can talk when you get to your hotel."

"I will and we will."

"Have a good meeting with the Ambassador."

"Thanks. Night babe."

"Bye," she whispered. She pressed the phone to her chest, wanting to hold him close to her for a moment more before she set the phone down on the nightstand. It was the right thing to do, she reminded herself, the only thing to do.

She set her phone on vibrate and placed it on the nightstand then stretched out on the bed. Within moments, sleep held her in its grasp.

When her eyes flickered open hours later the room was bathed in the glow of the setting sun. She blinked, confused. Nothing looked familiar. By degrees, her sense of place returned. She was in Baton Rouge. Home.

She pulled herself up into a sitting position and glanced around her space. Her reality crashed around her. Lightly she shook her head and pushed up from the side of the bed. She picked up her cell phone to discover that Traci called while she was asleep. She listened to the voice message and then called her back.

The phone rang several times before Traci answered in a rushed voice.

"Hey, it's me," Jacqueline said. "Everything okay?"

"Yeah, just a little crazed. The movers are here."

Jacqueline's heart thumped. "Any problems?"

"No, just trying to make sure they don't break anything while they pack." She blew out a breath. "How was the flight?"

"Uneventful. Listen, Traci, I know I'm asking a lot from you and I know how much you're against this. I want you to know I really appreciate everything you're doing for me."

Traci was silent for a moment, and Jacqueline listened to the sound of strange male voices in her soon-to-be vacated condo.

"I know you do," she finally said. "Everything okay on your end?"

"Yeah. I woke up from a nap and for a minute I didn't have a clue where I was," she said, pushing lightness into her voice.

"I better get back to the movers. I'll…uh, call you."

Jacqueline blinked back the sting of tears in her eyes. "Okay. And Traci…"

"Yes?"

"Thank you."

"You're my sister, J. And…I would do anything for you. You know that."

"I know. We'll talk later." She disconnected the call and sat perfectly still for several moments. A chapter of her life was coming to an end. When she'd purchased the L.A. condo she was sure that she had finally put down roots, that she would have a place to call home when she returned from her innumerable trips around the world. She'd rented a small apartment in New York, which is where she would go when she left Baton Rouge after the wedding. Some of the best doctors in the world that specialized in treating her condition were in New York. Although there wasn't much more that could be done, save for the one alternative she refused to pursue, they were making strides every day. *Strides equaled hope.*

Resolved, she set the phone down, reached for the remote, turned on the television and surfed to CNN. There was the usual spate of uprisings around the world: bombings, fire, famine and government coups. Newscasters were never at a loss for tragedy to feed the public. And then her brother's image was on the screen as he alighted from his car in front of the Lawson mansion.

"Senator Branford Lawson has returned to his roots, and not just for a good home-cooked meal but for the wedding of his daughter Dominique, twin sister to Desiree who was married last year. The nuptials are set for tomorrow afternoon and all of the Who's Who of Louisiana and beyond will be in attendance. Desiree

Lawson will marry Spence Hampton. Many of you may remember the eldest sister Lee Ann Lawson married Jr. Senator Preston Graham several years ago. And of course there is perennial bachelor and bad boy of the family, Rafe Lawson, and the youngest Lawson, Justin, who recently passed the bar. There will be no press at the event, but we do hope that the Camelot family of the South will share some of the pictures with us. In other news…"

Jacqueline released a sigh of relief. If she thought for a moment that the lure of the Lawson spotlight had dimmed at all, that idea was out of the window. At least she didn't have to worry about the press tomorrow.

Chapter 6

The wedding was scheduled for two o'clock. Jacqueline felt as if it were her own. Her nerves were frazzled. She'd been up with the sun, rehearsing over and over how she would act, what she would say when she saw her family again, how they would receive her. It was Lee Ann who'd sent the invitation but if it had family support she had no idea. The family was unaware that she was coming as she'd never RSVP'd since she had no intention of attending the reception, only the ceremony. She would see her family at the church and then be on her way.

The church was halfway across town and on a Saturday afternoon traffic would be heavy. Fighting off a bout of light-headedness, she gathered her nerves, her gift and purse and headed down to the lobby where a cab was waiting for her at the curbside.

She settled herself in the cab, leaned her head back against the seat and closed her eyes. Fatigue swept through her, making her limbs feel like wet spaghetti. She opened her eyes and stared out the window as the city of Baton Rouge spread out in front of her. Familiar sights brought back memories of happier times; the old Chelsea movie theater, Teddy's Juke Joint and Juban's Restaurant, one of her favorites. There were dozens of new businesses, boutiques and outdoor cafés as well that reminded her of how long she'd been gone.

The cab came to a barricade a block away from the church. An officer approached the car.

The driver lowered his window. The security officer poked his head in and looked inside. "Do you have an invitation, ma'am?"

"Yes." She opened her purse and took out the gold-embossed invitation and handed it to the officer.

"You're good to go." He handed the invitation back to her. "Pull up to the next intersection," he directed the driver before pulling the barricade aside.

"This is a really big deal," the driver said, slowly driving the car forward.

"Seems so." Jacqueline peered out of the window at the montage of guests that were alighting from their cars and entering the church. Police presence was everywhere. And there was no shortage of Secret Service, clearly distinguished by their earbuds and dark glasses; for her brother and brother-in-law's benefit, she concluded.

The cab driver went as far as he could go. "I'll have to let you out here, miss."

"Of course. Thank you." She checked the price on the meter and paid the fare, adding a nice tip. Willing herself to remain calm, she slid on her wide dark glasses and stepped out of the cab. For several moments she stood on the sidewalk, debating her decision to come when there was a sudden flurry of activity. All heads turned to the long, white stretch limo that was gliding to a stop in front of the church.

Jacqueline's heart thumped.

The driver hurried around and opened the door. Within a moment Lee Ann stepped out, followed by her sister Dominique and Zoe Beaumont, a longtime friend of the family. The ladies were dressed in exquisite dresses in varying lengths of a brilliant teal-blue. Their hair was pulled back from their faces, and behind the left ear of each was a single white lily à la Billie Holiday. And then the bride. Desiree stepped from the car, assisted by the driver. Those who were privileged to see her get out from the car took a collective gasp. She was a vision of perfection in pearl-white organza. A fitted gown that fishtailed at her ankles with jeweled insets at the bodice and down the entire back of the gown. Her face was obscured by her veil that sparkled with tiny jewels and shone like diamonds in the afternoon sun and the train rivaled that of the Princess of Wales.

Her bridesmaids lifted her train and followed her into the church.

Jacqueline folded herself in with the invited guests, found a seat on the bride's side of the church and waited for the ceremony to begin.

At the head of the church was the proud groom, Spence Hampton. Jacqueline could see how her niece had fallen for the handsome groom. He looked like he was ready for the cover of *GQ* in his black tux. And then the music began.

First came Lee Ann and Rafe, followed by Dominique and Justin then Zoe and a man she didn't recognize. Jacqueline's heart filled with pride as she looked at her nieces and nephews.

There was a pause as the bridal party took their places at the front of the church and then the wedding march began. The gathering rose to their feet in honor of the bride and the poignant organ music filled the cavernous walls of the church. The back door was opened by two ushers and the gorgeous bride, accompanied by Branford, stood in the threshold. Branford gazed down at Desiree and murmured something to her, a warm smile on his face. She slightly nodded her head and they took the long, slow walk down the aisle.

Jacqueline's heart thundered as they drew closer and Branford's dark eyes momentarily landed on her. An instant of recognition followed by disbelief darkened his features. He lifted his chin and continued down the aisle never missing a beat.

The forty-minute service, to Jacqueline, was surreal. She barely heard a word. Her thoughts scurried in disarray. All she could see was the look that her brother had thrown her way. It blocked out everything else.

And then the bridal party was walking back down the aisle. The new husband and wife glowed with the love that gleamed from their eyes for each other. The immediate family followed, beaming with smiles and waving and nodding at the guests who flanked them. Branford was mere footsteps away from her. He hesitated a moment, reached toward her and gently tugged her into the aisle.

He pulled her close, holding her by the elbow, never losing the proud father expression as he spoke to her from between clenched teeth. "What are you doing here?"

Jacqueline kept her face averted from prying eyes behind her dark glasses and wide-brimmed hat that swept as far as her shoulders and dipped low over her eyes.

"I came to see my niece get married."

"No one invited you, I'm sure of that."

They stepped out of the church into the blazing afternoon and the throng of enthusiastic guests.

"Lee Ann invited me."

His head snapped toward her. His jaw clenched. "I won't have you causing any problems."

They descended the stairs.

"Give your congratulations and then I want you gone. You drew the line between us years ago, Jacqueline."

He turned toward her. His eyes burned with something she couldn't quite place; anger, disappointment, hurt, she couldn't be sure.

Her chest tightened in pain. What made her think anything could be different between them, even after all this time? She didn't, not really. Yet, there was a part of her that held out a thin thread of hope. He'd just snapped it in half.

"Don't worry, brother dear, I have no intentions of being anything other than cordial. This is Desiree's day." She gently pulled away from his grip and continued down the steps.

The wedding photographers were setting up the bride and groom for pictures in front of the limos.

"Aunt Jacquie?"

She turned toward the sound of her name. She blinked back the sudden rush of tears that filled her eyes and was thankful for the dark glasses. Her heart thrummed in her chest.

"Rafe." She extended a hand to him. She pressed her lips tightly together to keep them from trembling.

He stepped up to her, tall, and what any woman would call dashing. There was an aura about Raford Lawson that set him apart from other men. He had the unquestionable charisma of his father, the looks of a movie star and the demeanor and behavior of a bad boy that was barely contained.

He took her hand and pulled her close for a hug. Then held her at arms length.

"My God, I can't believe you're actually here. Lee Ann said she'd sent you an invitation, but we didn't hear from you." His smile could melt the ice caps. He hugged her again. "How long has it been? A decade at least." He studied her from beneath his long black lashes. "Has Daddy seen you?"

She swallowed and looked up at him. "Yes."

The corner of his mouth curved slightly upward. "Since you've managed to get beyond the first gauntlet, let's cozy up with the rest of the family."

"Rafe...I don't want to cause any problems with your father. I only wanted to see Desi get married. I did that. So I'd better go." She lifted the Tiffany shopping bag that held the gift. "Give this to Desi for me."

His grinned turned wickedly mischievous. "I absolutely will not. You can give it to her yourself. Besides, what's a family wedding without a little dust up?" He took her arm and hooked it through the bend in his. "Think of me as your personal escort for the day, unless you came with one of your own."

"No. I didn't." She peeked up at him and the halo of a smile teased her full mouth.

"Perfect." He patted her hand. "Come, let's go kiss the bride."

The photographer was calling for the bridal party for photos as Rafe and Jacqueline approached.

The three sisters recognized her simultaneously and their squeals of delight, kisses and hugs made her realize like a punch to the gut exactly how much she had missed them all. She knew if she started crying she wasn't going to stop.

The questions from her nieces came fast and furious. *When had she arrived? How long was she staying? No hotels, stay at the house. Have you seen Daddy? What did he say? Why didn't you let us know you were coming?*

She didn't have the chance to answer one question before another was launched at her. She had no idea what kind of reception she was going to get, but she never expected this in a million years.

"I'm so glad that you're here, Aunt Jacquie," Desiree said, holding her hands in her own soft ones. She turned to her right. "This is my husband," she said, blushing as the words slid for the first time from her polished lips. "Spence Hampton. Spence, my Aunt Jacquie."

Jacqueline extended her hand. "Welcome to the family," she said. "You're a very lucky man."

"I know." He kissed Desiree's cheek. "Glad to finally meet you."

The photographer interrupted the gathering to finish up the pictures before they headed off to the reception at the Lawson mansion.

Jacqueline stepped back out of camera range. Branford took several pictures with the bride and groom and his children. She stood well out of the way to ensure that she wouldn't be asked to step in for a family shot and possibly get into a face-off with her brother. It was best that she leave while she had the chance. She'd accomplished what she'd come for, to see her family for perhaps the last time.

She turned to leave and began weaving her way through the crowd of guests. She'd just made it to the outskirts of the crowd when someone grabbed her arm.

"Where are you going?"

She glanced over her shoulder at Rafe. "I…was heading back to my hotel."

"You're coming to the reception. As my 'date.' I don't take kindly to *no*. I think you should remember that about me."

"Rafe…really…"

"Come. We'll go in my car. Besides, you need to give Desi and Spence their wedding gift," he added, lowering his gaze in the direction of the bag in her hand.

She'd all but forgotten about her gift for the newlyweds. "I could just give it to you and let you do the honors on my behalf."

"Oh, no. You won't be getting off that easy." He leaned down toward her ear. "Don't worry, I'll be close." He gave her that smile that women were hard-pressed to resist—even aunts.

"All right," she conceded on a breath. "I'll go—for Desi's sake and because it's so damned hard to tell you no." She playfully swatted his arm and allowed Rafe to lead her to his waiting car.

"Didn't you come in the limo with the rest of the bridal party?" she asked, finding it curious that he'd driven his car.

He opened the passenger door. "I never leave myself at the mercy of someone else."

She slid onto the plush leather, looked up at him and shook her head in delight. Typical Rafe.

"So, let's make small talk," Rafe said, once he was behind the wheel.

Jacqueline slightly angled her head in his direction, biting back a smile. "Fine. Lovely weather."

Rafe chuckled. His eyes creased at the corners. "How's the weather where you've been?"

Her smile faded. She glanced away. "Sunny and warm," she said quietly.

"I follow your stories from time to time."

"Do you?"

"Of course. You're famous." He turned to her and grinned. "I've always admired you, Aunt J. I've admired that you were always your own woman and never tried to use the Lawson name to further your career. You did it all on your own."

"How are things with the family?" she asked, steering the conversation away from herself.

Rafe gave a slight shrug of his left shoulder. "Spreading their wings. Lee Ann is in D.C. most of the time with her husband, heir apparent, and her big-time political job. Desi is now married off to the resident entrepreneur. Justin is finishing up law school. Dad is… Dad. He and I are still at odds, but that's just the way things are."

Jacqueline noted the hint of wistfulness in his voice. She knew how difficult Branford could be, how unreachable his expectations were for his children, and for Rafe in particular. Rafe, like her, was a free spirit, uninhibited and unwilling to bend to the demands of others. They listened to their own drummer and that was something Branford Lawson had been unable to tolerate.

Jacqueline glanced out of the window and the Lawson mansion loomed in front of her. The massive manicured lawn glistened like polished emeralds in the sun. Cars and limos were already pulling up along the winding driveway, assisted by red-vested valets. Music could be heard floating in the late-afternoon air. Her pulse quickened. Her last visit had been fraught with harsh words and ugly accusations. She'd stormed out vowing never to return and she had kept her promise to herself—until now.

She pressed her lips tightly together and willed her heart to slow its rapid thudding. She gripped her purse between her fingers. The trip, seeing everyone again, the secrets—they were all beginning to take a physical toll. She felt light-headed and her limbs felt weak, all the precursors to another episode. She should not have come.

Rafe placed his hand on her fisted ones. "We're here," he said softly, then looked at her more closely. "Are you all right, Aunt J? You're sweating and the air is on high. Are you coming down with something?"

She blinked rapidly to push away the veil that had begun to descend in front of her. "No. I'm fine." She forced a smile and turned to him in a brief assurance. She wouldn't pass out if she continued to chant to herself.

His gaze moved slowly over her pinched expression. "I'll stay close. I promise." He leaned across the gears and kissed her damp cheek then hopped out and came around to open her door, not waiting for a valet. He extended his hand to help her to her feet.

Jacqueline gripped his hand as she stood and the ground seemed to shift beneath her. She drew in a breath. "The gift," she managed.

Rafe released her, opened the back door and took out the package. He bent his arm and she slid her hand through. He pulled her close and they walked, arm in arm to the main entrance.

Chapter 7

Branford had spared no expense, from the massive white-and-gold embroidered tents that dotted the landscape, to the food that could easily feed a small country, the bands, the hovering waiters, the flowers, the liquor and the laundry list of the Louisiana elite.

Jacqueline had almost forgotten what an affair at the Lawson home could entail. She walked across the front lawn, her face still shielded by her wide hat.

"Let's get you something cool to drink," Rafe offered.

"You really don't have to babysit me, Rafe. I'm sure there are plenty of your admirers that you could squire around."

He pressed his hand to his chest. "Oh, you wound me, Aunt J."

She grinned. "I doubt that. Go on, I'll be fine."

He walked her to an available seat. "I'll get your drink. Wait here."

Jacqueline lowered herself into the upholstered chair beneath a tent and set the gift on the table. A wave of relief rolled through her to be off her feet. She looked around at the swelling gathering. There were more than a few faces that she recognized from her former life in Baton Rouge, but she made no effort to identify herself.

She watched Rafe's approach and was tickled to see that her prediction was true. He was stopped at least a half dozen times by exquisitely clad ingenues who vied for his attention. Being the Southern gentleman that he was, he gave each one a moment of his time and plenty of his charm before returning to her with a glass of champagne.

"Seems it's all we have at the moment," he said, handing her the flute.

She gratefully took the shimmering golden liquid and took a small sip, then another. It glided across her tongue and burst in gentle bubbles in her throat before slowly moving onward like a caress. She couldn't begin to imagine how much Branford had spent on this champagne. It was like a magic elixir.

"Thank you."

"Sure. Do you want to stay here or—"

"Rafe!"

He glanced over his shoulder. Dominique was hurrying toward them, smoothly maneuvering around the guests and tables and waiters.

"Whew," she breathed, "never realize how many people you know until there's free food and liquor." She emitted a devilish laugh. Her face was aglow. "Desi wants pictures, big brother," she said, sliding her hand around Rafe's waist. "It's so good to see you, Aunt J. And I know how much this means to Desi that you're here."

"I'm glad I came."

"You must join us for a real family photo," Rafe said, tossing back the last of his champagne. His dark eyes sparked with mischief. "The old man will be apoplectic."

Jacqueline couldn't help but laugh. "You'd enjoy that wouldn't you?"

"I think I would."

Jacqueline shook her head. "This is Desi's day and I'm not going to do anything that would put a damper on it. And me getting within ten feet of my brother would do just that."

Dominique studied her for a moment. "Whatever happened between you and my father was a long time ago. Today if none other is the perfect time to bury whatever it is that's between you."

"I wish it was that simple, Dom."

"It's about Uncle David," Rafe stated more than asked.

Jacqueline's lips tightened.

"No one ever talks about it," Dominique said softly. "But it's like a cloud that continues to linger long after the storm is over."

"Maurice blames him," Rafe said, referring to their cousin and David's only son.

Jacqueline slightly lowered her head then looked up at them taking each one in. "I didn't come here to open old wounds," she said slowly. She pushed herself up and stood in front of them. "Go and take your pictures. Your sister and her new husband are waiting. I'm going to put this gift inside and see if I can remember where the restroom is." She offered them a smile.

"Okay, but don't you dare disappear," Dominique warned. "We have catching up to do." She took Rafe's hand and they strolled off toward the gazebo on the far side of the property where the wedding party was assembling.

Jacqueline picked up the package and started toward the main house. There had to be at least two hundred people there and cars were still coming.

She took the three steps up onto the sweeping porch. The wide front doors stood open in welcome. If she thought for a moment that the outside was breathtaking, the interior was equally as magnificent. The banisters were wrapped in white gauze and trimmed with lilies. In the center of the floor was a massive ice sculpture of an entwined couple, trimmed all the way around in a bed of oysters on the half shell couched in ice.

The floors gleamed enough to see one's reflection. Long white linen tables lined the left wall and were piled high with gifts. The opposite side was set up with the same upholstered chairs as outside, arranged for intimate conversations. The entire space was draped from the top of the cathedral ceiling with sheer white and gold fabric that gave the impression of stepping into a wonderland.

Jacqueline placed her gift on the table on the pile with the others.

"Appetizer, ma'am?"

Jacqueline turned to the young waitress who carried a silver-toned platter of caviar and lobster dip on imported crackers with garnish.

Her stomach tumbled in response. She hadn't eaten and she'd had that glass of champagne. Bad combination, even more so for her.

She took the proffered plate and embossed napkin and added several of the delicacies to the plate.

There was apparently a small band down on the lower level that was playing music more appropriate for the much younger set. The music that drew her was coming from out back. She took her plate, added a skewer of shrimp and peppers and followed the pull of music out on the back lawn.

Desiree and her brand-new husband, Spence, were on the center of the raised dance floor, swaying to the music with eyes only for each other.

For a moment, Jacqueline was Desi on that dance

floor and wrapped in her arms was Raymond. They moved, as they always did, like one perfect note. She inhaled his familiar scent, explored the curve of the hard lines of his back, felt the heat of his body pressed against hers. Her throat constricted and she blinked away the vision. But everywhere that she looked couples rejoiced in the magic of love and togetherness, the forever promise of a relationship. Her own eyes burned but she couldn't seem to look away, wishing from the pit of her soul that things could be different.

But she had not made the vows to Raymond, at least not out loud. He was not bound to her in sickness and in health, for richer for poorer. He was still free to move on with his life. She refused to be the pre-existing condition.

Branford spotted his sister on the far side of the lawn, standing out like a lone star among the heavens. Although he continued to remain fully engaged in conversation, he still managed to keep an eye on Jacqueline. Seeing her, so suddenly, after a decade had unsettled him in a way that he would never have expected. Although she looked as stunning as always, he noticed the weariness around her eyes and the slight downward curve of her mouth. Much like him, Jacqueline always had a reason for doing everything. Nothing was done on a whim without some benefit at the end. Why was she really here? She hadn't attended Lee Ann's wedding, although he was certain that his children sent her an invitation. Why now?

A part of him wanted to talk to her, really talk to her the way they'd sometimes done during their youth. The last time they'd been in the same space together had opened an ugly chasm of recriminations that neither was willing to cross. She accused him in no uncertain terms in the tragic suicide of their brother. She shook the letter that David had left behind for his son, Maurice, to find in his face. *You drove him to it! He needed you and you abandoned him. You were the one person that could have saved him but you were more interested in your own miserable life and career than your own family. I will never, as long as I have a breath, forgive you. You selfish, sanctimonious bastard!*

It was the last thing she'd said to him before she tore out of the study, past the family and close confidantes who'd gathered at the house to mourn the loss of David Lawson.

There wasn't a day that had gone by since that awful afternoon that he had not relived that confrontation. He could have told her. He could have tried to explain. His pride and his promise would not let him. What stabbed him in the heart that many thought he didn't have, was that his own sister would think so little of him.

He'd learned to live with her disdain. He'd learned to live with losing his nephew Maurice to the same acrimony. Instead of it being a searing pain, it had dulled to an intermittent throb. Until now.

Chapter 8

The sun was beginning to set over the festivities, but the bands played on, the food and liquor flowed and the merriment continued.

Jacqueline could feel the fatigue begin to envelope her, from the balls of her feet, up through her limbs, to the lightness in her head and the almost unbearable need to curl into a ball and rest. She needed to leave but then remembered with a jerk in her chest that Rafe brought her here in his car and she had no transportation back to the hotel.

Frowning, she glanced over heads and shoulders and between bodies to see if she could spot Rafe or perhaps Dominique.

Dominique was in deep conversation with Senator

Long. Lee Ann, she did not see. As she moved between bodies, she felt as if she was moving in slow motion. Dark spots began to dance in front of her eyes. She breathed in deeply, trying to push oxygen to her brain and slow the sensation of being on the precipice of falling from a high place.

"Aunt J, are you all right."

Suddenly a strong arm was around her waist, an instant before she felt her knees give way.

"Y—es." She squeezed her eyes shut for a minute. "Too much champagne."

"Let's sit down."

She clasped Rafe's arm. "I know this is an imposition, but could you get a car service. I…" Her heart raced so rapidly she could barely breathe. "I need to get back to my hotel."

Rafe's expression tightened with concern. "I'll take you."

"No, really…"

"I brought you. I'll take you."

She looked up at his concerned face and held back tears of fear and gratitude. "Thank you," she murmured.

"I'll be right back. Wait here. Please."

She nodded.

Jacqueline watched the festivities continue to shift into a higher gear. The music and noise became deafening. Her head pounded. She gripped her purse to be able to hold on to something tangible to ground her.

Just breathe, she silently chanted. Soon you will be

in bed. You can close your eyes. The fatigue and waves of nausea will ease. Breathe.

"Let's get you out of here."

Rafe was standing above her with his hand extended. Gratefully, she placed her hand in his and slowly stood. Within moments, he had her fastened in her seatbelt in his car.

"Where are you staying?"

"The Belle."

He put the car in gear and they headed out.

They remained quiet for the ride to the hotel. The space between them filled with soft music from the local radio station, interspersed with advertisements about an upcoming music festival. Rafe snatched periodic looks at Jacqueline. Her expression was set. Her lids often drifted close as if her lashes dragged them unwillingly down. And Rafe noticed, for the first time, that beneath the well-applied makeup, the toned body and designer outfit, his aunt wasn't well.

He eased the car along the winding lane to the main entrance of the hotel. A doorman quickly approached the driver side.

"Welcome to the Belle. Are you guests or visitors?"

"Both," Rafe answered. "Ms. Lawson is a guest. Can you park the car, please?"

"Rafe, there's no need for you to stay."

He threw her a look. "I intend to make sure you get settled."

He got out of the car, came around and opened her

door. The valet was summoned and he got behind the wheel and pulled off as Rafe walked with Jacqueline inside.

"Where is your card key?"

She glared up at him and one glance told her that he would not be denied. If he handled his own aunt this way, she could only imagine the sway he had with the women in his life. She pursed her lips, opened the snap on her purse and took out her card key. She handed it to him.

"What floor?"

"Ten," she muttered like an errant child.

He took her arm and they walked to the elevator.

"You really don't have to do this," she tried again as they waited for the elevator to descend.

"Probably not, but I am anyway."

The bell tinged and the shiny doors slid open. Rafe pressed ten. They rode in silence. Rafe loosened his bow tie and let it hang from around his neck. He opened the top two buttons of his tuxedo shirt and visibly relaxed. Jacqueline smiled to herself.

The doors opened. She stepped out and led the way down the hall to her suite. Rafe stepped around her and slid the card key through the slender slot.

Jacqueline stepped across the threshold and felt the room shift. A wave of nausea rose from the bottom of her stomach. Black dots danced in front of her eyes. She reached for the table to steady herself.

"Aunt J!"

Chapter 9

Jacqueline could hear voices and movement coming to her from a distance. She felt as if she was pulling herself up from a deep cushiony cocoon. She wanted to go back but the voice kept tugging at her.

"Can you hear me?"

"Aunt J?"

"She's coming around."

There was something covering her mouth and nose. She tried to get it off. Someone grabbed her hand.

"That's oxygen to help you breath," an authoritative voice said.

She blinked away the last of the shadows. The room came into a hazy kind of focus. Rafe was standing over her, a worried smile on his face.

"The EMS is here, Aunt J." He sat on the side of the bed. "We're going to take you to the hospital."

Panic gripped her. She tugged her arm away from the EMS worker that was taking her pulse and snatched the oxygen mask from her face. "No. No hospitals."

"Aunt J, you collapsed. You've been out for almost ten minutes. Something is wrong. You're going to the hospital to let them check you out."

"It's nothing," she said feebly. "The jet lag, the heat. That's all. I'm fine." She tried to get up and found that she didn't have the strength and that's when the tears sprung from her eyes.

"It's all right, Aunt J. I won't leave you. I promise. Let's get going," he instructed the EMS team.

She gripped Rafe's wrist with a strength that surprised him. "Don't tell anyone. No one must know," she said, her tone almost desperate.

Rafe's brows drew together as he looked at the desperate determination in her eyes. Whatever was wrong was more than heat exhaustion and she knew it. "I won't say anything," he finally conceded.

She exhaled a sigh of relief.

Of course Rafe had once dated the Chief of Emergency Services and after a brief conversation, Jacqueline was whisked in, triaged and was being examined by the Chief herself.

"I'm Doctor Ravenell," the stunning woman said. She could have easily passed for a model. "How are you feeling now?" She held Jacqueline's wrist in her hand and listened to her pulse.

"Better."

"Hmm. Have you had fainting spells before?"

"Yes."

"Your pulse is weak and a bit thready. I want to run some test but first, let me ask you a few questions."

Rafe sat in the waiting area, his long legs sprawled out in front of him. Several of the nurses walked by the glass-enclosed room just to get a peek at the hunk in the tuxedo. Rafe didn't notice. His thoughts were on his aunt. His gut told him something was seriously wrong and for whatever reason she didn't want anyone to know.

Growing up, his Aunt J was more like an older sister than an aunt. Being the youngest sibling of his father and with so many years between them, she was only ten years older than Rafe. They'd all been close once upon a time. Dominique idolized Jacqueline and swore she was going to be just like her fabulous, globe-trotting aunt. His cousin Maurice had been his best friend.

All that had changed. His jaw tightened. His father was at the center of it all, and he'd done nothing over the decade to right the wrongs.

"Rafe."

His head snapped up. Dr. Sylvia Ravenell stood in front of him.

"Hey." He jumped to his feet. "How is she?"

"We're going to admit her, Rafe." She paused for a moment, gauging her words. "Your aunt…is very ill."

His pulse drummed in his ears. "What do you mean very ill? What's wrong with her?"

She drew in a long breath. "I'll let her tell you. We're going to do some tests. I'm having her transferred to ICU on the Oncology floor."

His eyes widened in alarm. "Oncology…that's the cancer floor."

She reached out and gently held his arm. "Take it easy. It's also the floor where we can do specialized tests for blood disorders."

"So what are you saying, that she has…cancer?"

"No. I'm saying we're going to run some tests. Dr. Phillips will take over when we move her and he will be in touch with her doctors in California."

California? Is that where she'd been? Doctors? He shook his head to clear it then looked into her eyes. His voice was a low rumble. "Is he the best? That's all I want to know. Because if he's not, get the best in here. Money is no object."

"Trust me. He is the best. One of the best in the country."

He rocked his jaw back and forth then slowly nodded his head. "Can I see her?"

"They're moving her now. You can meet her up on the fourth floor in about a half hour. After she gets settled."

"I'm going with her. I don't want her to think that she's alone."

She saw that familiar look in his eyes. "Fine. Come with me."

They walked together back down the corridor to the triage unit. "I take it you haven't seen each other in a while."

"No. Not for about ten years or so," he murmured.

"Hmm. She's a very determined woman."

"Runs in the family."

"I remember well."

He glanced at her and noticed the shadow of a smile around her well-formed lips. He tried to remember why they didn't work out, but he couldn't.

They approached the area where Jacqueline was being treated. Dr. Ravenell pulled the curtain back. They'd already gotten her out of her clothing and had her hooked up to an IV. Jacqueline tried to smile when she saw Rafe.

"They're going to transfer you upstairs. Doc here said I can come along for the ride," he said, forcing a lightness into his voice.

"Thanks."

He came to stand beside her. He took her hand. "Everything is going to be fine, Aunt J."

She glanced away.

Two orderlies came into the space and began adjusting the bed and IV stand for transport. Rafe stood back while they worked then followed them for the trip to the fourth floor. Dozens of thoughts flew through his head while they rode the elevator in silence, none of them good. Why had she come back after all this time? How long had she known she was sick? Why didn't she want anyone to know? And most important, what the hell was wrong with her?

The wedding reception was finally winding down. The hired help was busy cleaning and packing up. Dominique and Spence had left about an hour earlier en route to their two-week honeymoon in Saint Tropez on the French Riviera and then a week in Acapulco.

The exhausted wedding party was gathered out back, shoes off, feet up, sipping on Cristal and sharing tidbits about the events of the day.

"What a day," Lee Ann said on a breath. She rested her head back against the chair.

"Bring back memories?" her husband, Preston, asked, squeezing her hand.

Lee Ann flashed him a loving smile. "It does," she said with a hint of something inviting in her voice.

"Where is Rafe?" Dominique asked, taking a quick look around. "I haven't seen him for hours."

"Probably off with one of his lady friends," Justin said.

"I haven't seen Aunt Jacquie either," Lee Ann added.

"Now that was a surprise," Dominique said. "I had no idea that she would actually show up."

"Do you know if she and dad spoke?" Lee Ann asked looking around at the gathering.

Dominique shook her head. "I don't think so."

"I wish that they would settle the differences between them," Lee Ann said. "What happened with Uncle David was a long time ago. When it's all said and done we're family."

Murmurs of agreement moved around the group.

"I thought Maurice would have come," Dominique said.

"Why?" Justin asked.

She turned to her younger brother. "Dad went to see him about a month ago."

"He did?"

"Dad doesn't know that I found out."

"How did you find out? And why didn't the rest of us know?" Lee Ann asked, sitting up.

"Dad and Rafe went to one of Melanie's parties. Maurice was there."

Lee Ann's eyes widened. "What? Is he all right?"

Dominique told them about Maurice's injury and that he'd left the Navy SEALs. He was at Sag Harbor resting and recuperating and had taken up with a woman named Layla, the massage therapist. There was a big blow up the night of the party between Dad, Rafe and Maurice. Apparently, Dad went to see Maurice in New York and patched things up.

"Wow," Lee Ann said softly when Dominique had finished.

"So there is hope for the old man after all," Justin quipped.

"Maybe he's softening around the edges with age," Preston offered.

"Maurice and Aunt Jacquie blamed dad for what happened with Uncle David," Lee Ann said. "I know Dad can be hard and unbending, but it was and still is difficult for me to believe that he would turn his back on his family. I was always torn between the father I know and what my cousin and aunt accused him of."

"We'll never know the truth if Dad won't talk about it," Justin said.

"Your father is a man of principles," Preston interjected. "He's a man who sticks by his beliefs. He's one of the few in the senate that can never be swayed by pressure or politics or outside influences. Those are the qualities that have made him an unbeatable legislator. There are many who hate him but they also respect him. I'm sure that whatever transpired all those years ago between him and his brother he never took lightly and he's carried it with him all these years."

Lee Ann turned to her husband, her eyes filled with love. *Thank you,* she mouthed.

"Well, if Dad would go so far as to seek out Maurice to make peace, maybe there is hope for him and Aunt Jacquie, too," Dominique said.

"Maybe that's why she came back," Justin said.

Chapter 10

"I know this is a lot that I'm asking you Rafe, but you have to promise me that you won't say anything. As soon as I'm strong enough, I'll be moving to New York. They have some new treatments there that the doctors say may help."

"You don't have to do this."

"Yes, I do."

"Why?" he ground out. "What is it about this family that makes us all so self-fucking righteous!" He ran his hand across the smooth dark waves of his head in frustration.

Jacqueline briefly shut her eyes and if she didn't know better she'd swear it was her brother standing next to her bed and not her nephew. She opened her eyes, stretched out her hand to halt his pacing beside her. "Listen to me, Rafe, you of all people know that I am my own woman. This is my life and I have to live it the way I see fit." She thought of Raymond and her stomach tumbled. "And sometimes…unfortunately, that means being selfish and not doing what others want you to do. But you do it because you know that it's best for you."

Rafe stared down at her, saw the unwavering determination in her eyes that was so much like his own and his father's. He did understand. For his entire life he'd lived on the edge, bucking authority and tradition, doing what was right for him much to the dismay of family and friends.

He heaved a heavy sigh. "All right," he finally relented. "If this is what you want. But I plan to be here every day until you get out of that bed."

She gave him a grateful smile. "Thank you," she whispered.

A nurse entered the room. "I have to take some blood," she said, practically batting her eyes at Rafe.

Jacqueline bit back a smile. Rafe stepped aside.

"There's nothing more for you to do here tonight," Jacqueline said. "Go home and get some rest. I'm sure I'm in good hands."

"I'll be back first thing in the morning."

"I'm sure I'll be here," she tried to joke.

Rafe leaned down and kissed her warm forehead. He turned to the nurse and she nearly gushed. "Take good care of her."

"Oh, I will." He gave her a brief nod and the benefit of his winning smile. Her cheeks flushed crimson.

Rafe strode out of the hospital, cutting a devastating figure in his tux. He paid little to no attention to the appreciative and sometimes questioning gazes that were flashed his way as he headed for the exit.

Once behind the wheel of his car he allowed himself a moment to process what little that he knew. He hung his head as a wave of sadness coursed through him. It didn't have to be this way. It didn't.

He looked ahead and put the car in gear. Although he'd made a promise to his aunt, he wasn't sure how long he would be able to keep it or if he should and there was no one he could talk to about it.

Raymond put his cell phone down on the table. He'd been calling Jacqueline for hours and got nothing more than her voice mail. This was the second day with no word from her. Deep in his gut, the knot that had been there since before he took off for Indonesia had only tightened. Something was wrong. He knew it as sure as he knew his own name. And it had to do with Jacqueline.

Being thousands of miles and time zones away added to the frustration. If it was up to him he would get on the next plane back to the states and demand to know what was going on with her.

She had not been her vivacious self for months. He crossed the room and stood at the terrace door that opened onto the bustling city of Jakarta. He knew that she was hiding something from him. He just didn't know what it could be, or better yet, why.

He shoved his right hand into his pants pocket and pulled out the diamond ring that he'd been carrying around for weeks, waiting for the right moment. But things had been off between him and Jacquie lately and the right time never seemed to present itself. He stared at the sparkling diamond in his palm, set on a slim platinum band. The corner of his mouth lifted ever so slightly as he thought about how nervous he was the afternoon when he picked it up from the jeweler.

"Mr. Jennings," the jeweler had enthusiastically greeted him. "Your ring is ready."

Raymond felt like a kid getting his first car. Excitement mixed with raw nerves had beat inside his belly. But this was bigger than a first car. It wasn't only about him. He was preparing to change his life forever. For a woman.

The jeweler turned to the tray of drawers behind the glass counter and pulled one open. He lifted the box marked with Raymond's name. Reverently he placed the box on the table and slowly opened it, heightening the drama for drama's sake.

The ring was stunning. It sparkled as the light bounced off of the points making it appear to glow from underneath.

"All done to your specifications, Mr. Jennings. I know she will be very happy."

Raymond lifted the ring from the velvet casing and held it between two fingers. He would ask her tonight. That was the plan. He'd made reservations at their favorite restaurant. And after a wonderful meal, soft lights, good music and dessert he would pop the question.

He'd been so sure. He'd had it all worked out in his head. He could visualize the look of surprise and then joy on Jacqueline's face.

Raymond never envisioned himself as the marrying kind. He relished his freedom, his ability to do as he chose, pick up and leave on a whim. The women in his life had to understand and accept that or they were gone. He didn't do clingy and needy, which, unfortunately many of the women he'd bedded became. But Jacqueline was different. Right from the first night that they'd met, he knew she wasn't like all the others. She had no more interest in him than a loaf of bread. That intrigued him. Then meeting again half a world away, he knew that destiny had stepped in.

They became not only friends and then lovers but partners in the amazing life that they lived. Together they chronicled the world from the steps of the White House, to uprisings in the farthest corners of the world.

Jacqueline excited him in a way that he could not explain. She was fearless in the most dangerous of situations, daring to go where many of their crew refused, into the mouth of death and danger to get 'the money shot.' She was uninhibited in her opinions and equally uninhibited in bed. She never let him doubt what was on her mind and what she wanted. It's what he loved about her. She'd changed him in ways that he had not anticipated. He'd become settled. His hunger for something new and different was satisfied with Jacquie. He'd stopped looking for the next best thing. He'd found it with her.

Noise from the traffic below floated up to him. He squeezed the ring in his hand before putting it back in his pocket.

Why had he never told her that he loved her? Never said the words. He turned away from the terrace and stepped back inside. He knew. He'd never told her because there was that tiny corner of his heart that remained unsure about her feelings for him. She'd made it clear that her career was her life. Her freedom was like an elixir. And she wasn't willing to give that up. Even as he'd driven home with the ring burning a hole in his jacket pocket he wasn't sure that she would say yes. And he knew if he crossed that line with her, asked her that question, there was no turning back. Their relationship would be altered forever—one way or the other.

He was willing to risk a lot of things, bodily injury, incarceration, hunger, thirst, terrorist's bombings and even hostage situations. But he wasn't willing to risk losing Jacqueline.

So they'd had that lovely dinner. They'd talked and laughed and came home and made love until the sun rose and finally lulled them to sleep. And the ring remained in his pocket.

His cell phone rang and he quickly crossed the room and snatched it up from the table.

"Hello?"

"Ray, it's Matt."

Matthew Davis was his partner on the junket. More than that they were real friends. They had both attended Columbia University's School of Journalism and wound up competing for many of the same plumb assignments. Understanding that opportunities for young black male journalists were few, they opted to squash the competition and pool their talents. Once that hatchet was buried they became fast friends, finding a love for a good beer, a good basketball game and beautiful, intelligent women. Matt was the only one he'd confided in about buying the ring for Jacquie.

His spirits dipped. "Hey, Matt."

"Everything is all set up for the interviews this afternoon."

"Yeah, good."

"Don't sound so excited."

Raymond ran a hand across his face as if he could wipe the worry away. "Sorry, just distracted."

"Listen we're free for the morning. Let's take a ride, see some sights for a change."

Raymond chuckled halfheartedly. It was true. There was rarely time to actually see the hundreds of places that they'd traveled to. Most of their hours were spent working, negotiating and working some more. Maybe getting out for a while would take his mind off of why he hadn't heard from Jacqueline in two days.

"Yeah, why not. Give me about five minutes. I'll meet you in the lobby." He disconnected the call and tried Jacqueline one more time. Again he got her voice mail. He had one more day in Indonesia and then he would head home. Jacqueline had some explaining to do.

Chapter 11

"Ms. Lawson, I'm Dr. Phillips."

"Good morning."

He adjusted his half-framed glasses and flipped through the pages of her chart then focused his green eyes on her. "I spoke with your doctor in L.A. You've been on medication for about six months now."

"Yes."

"You have discussed your options?"

"Yes."

"Ms. Lawson, I have to agree with your doctor that the medication is not doing the job. The transplant could make you turn the corner. It's my opinion and the opinion of my team that it's the only alternative at this point. You're at a critical stage."

Jacqueline's throat went dry. She'd heard this all before but hearing it again was no easier.

"A family member would—"

"No! I don't want my family involved."

"But Ms. Lawson the chances for a full recovery…"

"I said, no, Dr. Phillips. I've been advised of all the options available to me. They…have some new medications in New York. I'm lined up for a trial. As soon as I'm able to leave here, I'm going to New York."

Dr. Phillips removed his glasses and slid them into the breast pocket of his bright white lab coat. He pushed out a long breath. He'd had his share of stubborn patients. He was accustomed to tantrums, denials, begging and even accusations, but it was rare that he found a patient that was unwilling to do whatever was necessary to save their own life.

"We'll do what we can to get your strength back and your levels up. You can do as you wish once you leave here, Ms. Lawson, but while you are here, you are under my care and supervision. And I will not in good conscience release you until I'm confident that you are up to traveling beyond this hospital room door."

She sighed in relief.

"Do you think you can at least follow my instructions until then?"

"I'll try," she said, a tentative smile on her lips.

"Good. I'll be back to check on you." He turned to leave.

"Thank you, doctor," she called out.

He stopped in the frame of the door, glanced at her for a moment before walking away.

She knew better than anyone what her last chance was—her brother Branford. How could she possibly go to him now after all the bad blood and recriminations that she'd hurled at him? Besides, when he'd had the chance to help their brother David, he didn't. And there was nothing to make her believe that he would do anything differently when it came to her.

Jacqueline reached for her cell phone that was on the nightstand next to her. She looked at the number of calls from Ray for the past two days. She squeezed her eyes shut against what he must be thinking. She'd gone over her decision a million ways from Sunday. She'd debated telling him what was going on with her, but knowing the outcome, she knew she could not do that to him, bind him to her in sympathy. She couldn't bear the look in his eyes. That would be worse than what she faced.

For months she'd hidden the truth from him. She attributed her growing fatigue and bouts of illness to travel, pressure from the job, anything but the truth.

One message after the other she deleted. It was better this way.

Steeling herself against what she knew would be Traci's barrage of questions, she dialed her number in L.A.

"In the hospital? What the hell?"

"Got back to my hotel after the reception and passed out. Nothing serious. They just want to check me out," she added, not wanting to alarm Traci more than necessary.

"Nothing serious! Jacquie, are you hearing yourself?"

Jacqueline rolled her eyes toward the ceiling. "I'm fine."

"No, you're not fine. J," she cried, her voice breaking with emotion. "Don't do this. At least let me come to Baton Rouge."

"Absolutely not. When I get out of here, which should be in a couple of days, I'm going straight to New York to start the trials. Did everything from the apartment get put into storage without any problems?" she asked, switching the topic away from her directly.

"Yes," Traci snapped. "Your apartment is empty of all of your personal belongings."

Jacqueline pushed out a breath. "Thanks."

"I mean have you taken one moment to imagine what Raymond is going to think when he comes back and the only thing left is a freaking note?"

"I have thought about it. I have imagined it. And it's ugly and it tears me up inside. But nothing, nothing could be worse for him than him watching…"

"J…sweetie. For once in your stubborn life lean on Ray. Let go of your stubborn pride and tell your family what's going on. Let someone help *you* for a change. You've spent your whole life trying to save the world by telling their stories through your photographs. It's your turn, sweetie."

Tears of fear and resolve slid over her lids. "I gotta go, Traci," she lied. "The nurse is here. I'll call you." She disconnected the call before Traci could react.

Jacqueline turned halfway on her side, her movements restricted by the IV in her arm. Was she really wrong?

Ray had been by her side in some of the most difficult situations. They'd had each other's back. They'd traversed deserts, and witnessed explosions, been caught in the melee of insurgencies, witnessed births in the jungle, and inaugurations in foreign lands. They'd slept in the best hotels and on mountainsides and along riverbeds.

She knew that Ray cared about her. He'd never said the words and neither had she, that wasn't who they were. To say the words would bind them in some way. And they were not souls to be bound.

But she should have told him, at least once, that she loved him. That was her only regret. Yet, if she had, this decision that she'd made would be even more painful.

The flight back to the States was longer than usual if that was possible, Raymond thought as he made his way through customs and then waited for his bags. He was bleary eyed, and bone tired. He still had been unable to reach Jacqueline and his emotions had veered from pissed off to worried. Matt had taken a flight out of Indonesia en route to New York for his next assignment, so Ray had traveled alone with his thoughts.

Finally he got his bags and hurried out to the taxi stand. A half hour later he was pulling up in front of Jacqueline's apartment complex. The sense of dread that he'd tried to keep at bay suddenly hit him with a sucker punch. His breathing escalated as he paid the driver and took his bags from the trunk. The feeling heightened as he approached her concierge desk and was stopped in midstep.

"Oh, Mr. Jordan? Did you forget something?"

Ray frowned in confusion. "Excuse me?"

"I was asking if you'd forgotten something."

"N-o. Why?"

The concierge flushed bright red. "I'm sorry. It's none of my concern, sir."

Raymond stared at him for a moment and then took off toward the elevator. His heart banged in his chest as the steel box made its slow ascent. The doors finally opened and he sprinted down the hall. Fumbling with the keys, he finally got it in the lock.

He pushed the door open and in one sweeping look at the yawning emptiness, his world crashed down around him.

Chapter 12

The thud of his bags dropping at his feet echoed in the space. Numb, he put one foot in front of the other, feeling as if he was in some kind of macabre dream. But it was real. The apartment was empty.

His stomach roiled. He gazed around in disbelief. Why? When? Maybe it wasn't what he thought. Maybe J had decided to get rid of her furniture and was ordering new stuff.

He ran toward the bedroom and threw the door open. Empty. He pulled open the closet door. Empty.

His temples pounded. He turned in a senseless circle. And then he saw it, an envelope propped up on the windowsill.

For a moment he simply stared at it. The answers to

the questions that raced through his head were in there. He knew it. He needed to know why she'd left him— like this—in this heartless way, like the years that they shared together meant nothing.

Gritting his teeth he crossed the room and lifted the pearly white envelope up by its edge and then he tore it into little pieces and let them fall like snow on the floor.

Whatever it said would never be explanation enough.

Raymond didn't remember the ride to his house. The familiar scenery passed by him unnoticed. Absently he wondered what she'd done with his things, the stuff he'd left at her place so that he'd feel like he belonged there instead of visiting like a guest. What did it matter anyway?

He paid the driver and dragged himself out of the cab. When he approached the path leading to his ranch-style house, his next door neighbor, Steve, stopped him.

"Hey, Ray. How's it going? How was the trip?"

"Long and tiring," he managed, in no mood for small talk.

"Well, hang on a sec. My wife signed for a package for you the other day. A big box. I'll get it."

He already knew what it was. She didn't miss a beat.

"Can it keep until tomorrow, Steve? I'm really exhausted."

"Yeah, sure. Hey, you okay, man?"

"Just tired. Long flight."

Steve nodded and watched him walk away.

* * *

Ray tossed his bags in a corner and went straight to the fridge and pulled out a bottle of beer. He drank it down like water and went for another one. He drank greedily. What he needed was something stronger. Something that could annihilate the feeling of disbelief and fury that had him on the edge of doing something ugly.

Before he realized what he was doing he'd hurled the bottle across the room. The sound of glass smashing reverberated in the space like a gunshot. The remnants of the beer dribbled feebly down the wall.

His cell phone rang deep in his pocket. He dug the phone out and it almost met the same fate as the bottle when he caught the name of the caller in the lighted face of the phone. Hesitating for a moment he debated whether to take the call. He depressed the phone icon.

"Where is she?" he barked into the phone.

"She doesn't want me to tell you, Ray. I'm breaking a promise to my friend. But…you need to know."

Rafe became a fixture in the hospital waiting room and in the corridors of the ward in the week that Jacqueline was a patient. She'd been moved from ICU and relocated to a private room on a regular floor. He'd made "friends" with many of the female staff so that neither he nor his aunt wanted for anything. They were more than happy to bring extra blankets or add extra helpings of food to her meal, refill her water, fluff pillows and "anything" that Rafe may have wanted to make his visits more comfortable. There was so much eye batting going on that air conditioning was hardly necessary, Jacqueline had joked with her nephew.

"I see you're getting your biting sense of humor back," Rafe said, as he pulled up a chair next to hers.

She'd been up and out of bed for the past two days. Her tests results had come back and were looking better than previously anticipated. The color had come back into her cheeks and her eyes were once again bright and all-seeing and, most important, her energy level was back. She was itching to leave.

Jacqueline crossed her long legs. "You have to admit, you have the ladies wrapped around your finger. I wonder if they would be quite as attentive to me if you weren't around."

The barest smile flickered around his mouth. "I was always taught, at my mama's knee, to treat the ladies with the utmost respect."

"And charm," she added.

His eyes sparked. "Well…that, too." He leaned back against the padded club chair he'd had brought to her room. "I spoke with Dr. Phillips. They plan to discharge you later today."

"Yes," she said on a breath. "Finally."

He leaned forward, rested his arms on his hard-muscled thighs and linked his fingers together. "You won't change your mind and stay?"

She slowly shook her head. "No. I'm going to New York."

"The family has been asking me about you, Dominique in particular. Her 'spidey' sense is picking up something. And you know Dom, once she get her hooks in something she won't let go. Lee Ann even called from D.C. asking had I heard from you."

"You haven't told them anything have you?"

"No. I told you that I wouldn't, and I'm a man of my word. But I have to tell you I don't care for lying to my family. We may not always get along but we're always up front with each other."

Jacqueline looked away. "I'm sorry to have put you in this difficult position. By tomorrow, I'll be gone and I won't be your burden any longer."

"You're not a burden. Why don't you understand that? You have people who care about you and would be there for you if you let them."

"It's not that simple."

"It is! If you let it."

She couldn't tell him the seriousness of her condition. All he knew was that she had a blood disorder. She'd done enough by involving him this far. That was never her intent. By tomorrow, she would be gone and life could go back to the way it was before she dropped into his lap.

"Let it go, Rafe," she said softly. She reached out and covered his tightened hands with her own. "I appreciate everything that you've done. But let it go. I'll be fine." She forced a bright smile. "Come, let's go for a walk to the solarium."

They got up and walked down the corridor. As usual the hospital floor was busy with doctors and nurses moving quickly and efficiently in and out of the rooms. They were approaching the nursing station and Jacqueline froze.

"What's wrong?" Rafe asked, immediately alarmed. He followed her line of sight.

Raymond was at the nurses' station being directed to Jacqueline's room. He turned and his gaze collided with hers.

"Ray," she uttered barely above a whisper.

"Who is that?" Rafe put his arm tighter around her slim waist.

"It's okay," she managed.

All of his emotions: anger, confusion, betrayal and fear tumbled on top of each other vying for position as he strode purposefully toward her. Seeing nothing and no one but the woman he'd come for.

"J." He breathed, grasping her shoulders then pulling her into his arms, as wave after wave of relief washed over him. "J," he whispered into her hair. "You could have told me. You didn't have to run."

She gave into the rush of joy that spread through her being back in the safety of his arms and fell into his embrace. Unbidden tears sprung from her eyes. "I'm sorry," she whispered. "I'm so sorry, Ray. I thought it was the only way."

"It's all right, baby. I'm here. I'm here." He kissed her hair, her cheeks her lips. "I'm here," he repeated against her pliant mouth.

Rafe cleared his throat. "I think you two are causing a scene."

Reluctantly, Raymond stepped back but refused to release her.

Jacqueline swallowed over the tightness in her throat. She grinned sheepishly. "This is my nephew. Rafe Lawson. Rafe, Raymond Jordan."

The two gorgeous men shook hands.

"I'm glad you're here," Rafe said.

Raymond looked deep into Jacqueline's eyes. "So am I."

"I'll, uh, leave you two to get reacquainted. I sense that there's a lot of talking that needs to be done." He leaned down and kissed Jacqueline's cheek. "See, I told you people love you," he whispered in her ear then stepped back and gave her a quick wink. "Good to meet you, Ray." He shook his hand again. "Take care of her."

"I intend to, whether she wants me to or not," he replied, more for Jacqueline's benefit than Rafe's.

"I guess Ray can take you back to your hotel," he stated more than asked.

"I got this," Raymond said.

"Good. Call me." He squeezed her hand then started off down the corridor, stopping along the way to make small talk with one of the nurses.

Of course Rafe could never tell his aunt that he knew

exactly what was wrong with her. It could cost one of the lovely nurses her job for having allowed him to see her chart. That knowledge and knowing what the only viable option for her full recovery was had tortured him for days. His hands were tied and he didn't like it one damned bit. Maybe, Ray would be able to love some sense into her. He saw how Ray looked at his aunt and he had a damned good feeling that Raymond Jordan was exactly what his aunt needed in more ways than one.

Chapter 13

"I suppose Traci told you," Jacqueline began, once they were settled in the quiet of the solarium. The morning sun gleamed against the floor-to-ceiling windows.

"She's your friend. And she's worried about you." He paused. "Why couldn't you tell me?"

"It's complicated."

"I'm listening."

She glanced away then turned to him. "The only way to possibly cure my aplastic anemia is with a bone marrow transplant. And the most viable person is my brother. My only other options are the clinical trials in New York."

He took in the information and measured his words before he spoke.

"We've been together for years now," he began. "We've been colleagues and lovers. But there has always been a wall between us, J. A wall that you put up. I know that it has to do with your family. And I know exactly who your family is."

She flinched.

"I've known for some time now. You forget that I'm an investigative journalist. I always thought that it was strange that you never spoke of your family or appeared never to want to have anything to do with them. I don't know the whole story, but I can't imagine that if your brother knew that you needed him, no matter what the rift is between you he would cross it."

She shook her head. "You don't know my brother."

"Then why don't you tell me what I don't know? For once, just tell me." He looked deep into her eyes, into her soul, touching her in a place that she'd kept locked away.

The weight of all that she'd been carrying finally gave way. The years of hurt and the self-imposed isolation broke free like a damn that burst its banks.

"There were three of us, Branford, my brother David and me. Branford and David were the stars of the family. Our father molded them, pushed them, compelled them to succeed. Branford entered politics. David finance. They both rose to the heights of their professions. But David…got in over his head. He made some bad decisions with his client's money. He was being investigated by the FTC. He told me he went to Branford for help and he refused."

She bit down on her bottom lip as those dark, frightening days replayed in her head.

"David's son, Maurice, found him. The gun was still warm in his hand. He'd left a note, saying how sorry he was but he saw no other way without the help that he needed. The help that only my brother could have given."

She blinked back the tears. "Maurice was devastated. It tore the family apart. Branford refused to talk to us about it. He never has." She sniffed.

"What happened with the investigation?" he asked after a long pause.

She frowned for a moment. "It…fizzled out."

"Just like that?"

"Yes…I suppose so."

"Did anyone ever think that perhaps Branford had something to do with that to maybe not tarnish your brother's name?"

"I…well…maybe. I don't know." In all this time she'd never even considered that.

"I'm sure if he did, it was at great cost to him on a lot of levels."

"But we don't know that he did."

"Believe me, reporters and the government don't simply go away because they're bored."

She drew in a long, thoughtful breath. "It doesn't change anything," she said none too convincingly.

"Only if you don't want it to."

"I can't go to him. I won't go to him. How could I after all this time and after all the ugliness?"

A sad smile tugged at the corners of his mouth. "As much as you have distanced yourself from your very famous family, you are more like them than you're willing to admit."

She sat up straighter in her seat. "What's that supposed to mean?"

"You're stubborn, focused, willful and determined not to bend or show your hand. You stand on ceremony and self-imposed principles. All those traits have made each of you a success in whatever you've undertaken." He waited a beat. "At some point, someone has to do things differently."

"Ms. Lawson…"

Jacqueline turned her attention toward the door of the solarium. The charge nurse was standing there. "Your discharge papers are ready."

Jacqueline beamed a smile. "Thank you." She turned bright eyes on Raymond. "Let's get out of here."

"You always loved the best hotels," Raymond quipped as he set down Jacqueline's bag and his own in the foyer.

"It's my answer to the nights of sleeping in tents and eating dried whatever when I'm on an assignment."

Raymond chuckled. "Bedroom in back?"

"Yes. Down this hall." She led the way. "You must

be exhausted," she said, turning to him. "You've been traveling for days on end."

As if on cue, he yawned. It seemed that he'd been in some state of "en route" for days now. His energy had been fueled by pure adrenaline. It was beginning to catch up with him as the anxiety since talking to Traci and finally seeing Jacqueline was easing back.

"Sorry." He chuckled. "I guess I am kind of tired."

"Why don't I run you a bath, and order room service?"

"That sounds too good." He crossed the room to stand in front of her. "But I can run my own bath. You just got out of the hospital."

"And I feel fine. Really. If I didn't they wouldn't have let me out. I assure you. Dr. Phillips was almost as single-minded as me," she said, her voice a combination of respect and reproach.

He brushed her pouty bottom lip with the pad of his thumb. "Why don't you join me?"

Her heart thumped. Her body instantly responded to the invitation, flooding with warmth. "I like that idea very much," she said, her voice growing thick.

Raymond jerked his head in the direction of the connecting bath. His half smile and the set of his eyes spoke volumes. He took her hands in his and slowly backed up toward the bathroom, completely captivated by the look of happiness in her eyes, but more important the need he saw hovering there. She *needed* him. And it was more than a physical need. He instinctively understood it. That's all he'd every wanted was for Jacqueline to let down her guard just for a moment and need someone other than herself.

They stepped into the all-white bathroom, grinning the way they used to before things got off-kilter with them, when Jacqueline started hiding the truth from him.

She went to the cabinet and took out her bath salts that she always had specially shipped from a tiny village in Kenya. She'd stumbled upon the group of women in an old stone building who'd made and packaged the salts when she was on assignment about five years earlier. She fell in love with the fragrances and the exquisite way her skin felt after a bath. Her greatest fear was that one day she'd place an order only to discover that the women had packed up and moved away or died off. Whenever that wayward thought ran through her head, she'd considered investing in them and making it a real business. But then her hectic life would get in the way and it would be one more thing added to her list of "want to."

Raymond turned on the water full blast in the huge soaker tub and Jacqueline liberally sprinkled in the fragrant salts. Quickly the room was filled with aromatic steam. Jacqueline sat on the edge of the tub and swirled the water around with her hand.

"I'm sorry," she said softly then looked around at Raymond through the moorlike mist. "I should have never left without…" She shook her head. "I handled the whole thing like I didn't have good sense."

"And you really packed up your entire apartment and put everything in storage?" he asked incredulously, still mystified as to how she'd pulled it all off. But Jacqueline was nothing less than resourceful.

She made a sheepish face. "I know. Stupid." She reached over and turned off the water. "All I could think about was that I didn't want you to be hurt by seeing me…sick." She swallowed. "It might…" her voice hitched…"it could get really bad, Ray."

He came to her and sat on the side of the tub. He lifted her chin with the tip of his finger. "It won't. And even if it does, I'm here every step of the way." His eyes grazed hotly over her face. Just don't shut me out, J."

She blinked rapidly to keep the tears at bay. Her smile wobbled. "I'll try."

"Try really hard." He grinned.

She reached for the buttons of his shirt and unfastened them one by one then eased the starched white linen over his muscled shoulders. For an instant, her breath stuttered when she saw the expanse of his chest and felt the warmth of his skin beneath her fingertips. The shirt was dropped to the floor. Then it was his turn.

His long fingers threaded through her hair at the nape of her neck sending thrilling shivers along the curve of her spine. He moved closer until his lips were no more than a breath away from hers.

Her lids fluttered closed as his mouth touched hers,

at first tentative and exploratory then by degrees reclaiming what had always been his.

He pulled her body to him. She moaned softly against his moist mouth while he parted her lips with a sweet swipe of his tongue.

"I've missed you," he groaned hotly against her exposed neck, pulling her loose-fitting peasant blouse over her shoulders to pool around her waist. "I've missed us." His head dipped to plant hot kisses along the swell of her breasts.

As she felt the fire rekindle within her she understood that it wasn't the physical act of making love that he missed. He missed *her*—the real her, the woman she'd always been with him and had run away from over the past months. And he missed the real intimacy that they'd always shared that she'd kept from him to make it easier for her to leave him. But no more. This was her man. He'd made that clear and it was only fair that she reciprocate.

Jacqueline slowly stood and pulled Raymond to his feet. She gazed up into his eyes. Her stomach fluttered to see his hunger for her hovering there.

"We are much too overdressed for a hot bath," she said, her voice thick and slow.

"I'm all for doing something about that." He reached around her, unfastened her bra and dropped it next to his shirt.

A wicked smile curved her mouth and she made quick work of freeing him from his slacks and boxers.

She wrapped her hand around his rising organ and gently brushed her finger back and forth across the sensitive head until he was full, rock solid and at attention.

Not to be outdone and, more importantly, to keep himself from exploding in her soft grip, Ray pulled off the rest of Jacqueline's clothing, tossed it aside and before she could utter a whimper, he'd scooped her up and placed her gently in the still hot and fragrant water. She pushed back to the far end of the tub to give him room to join her.

Jacqueline bent her knees while Raymond stretched his long legs out on either side of her then bent his knees as well before pulling her closer between his thighs. Her breasts bobbed teasingly above the waterline.

"Hey," he whispered in a teasing tone, his dark eyes filled with lust and love.

"Hey yourself." Her face flushed hot as she was suddenly shy around this man she'd known in the most intimate of ways.

He tenderly stroked her knee and then her leg. He reached for the lathering sponge on the side of the tub, squeezed a bit of shower gel on it and slowly began to massage and circularly work the lather up and down her legs and thighs. He teased her sex with featherlike swipes of the sponge, awakening the sensitive bud that bloomed amidst the closely cropped hair.

Jacqueline's heart pounded. She felt the blood hot and pulsing through her veins. Every caress of Raymond's was like another log being tossed into the fire. Soft whimpers floated atop the rising heat of the water.

"Turn around," Raymond said, his voice thick with need.

Jacqueline maneuvered her body so that her back was facing his front and she was nestled between his muscled thighs. She felt the hard rise of his phallus pressed against her back and a shiver ran through her.

"Lean back," he whispered in her ear.

She rested her head against his chest and let her eyes drift closed.

Raymond alternately dismissed the use of the sponge and used his hands instead to explore her body. Placing the gel in his palms he moved in slow motion up and down her body, cupping her breast, lathering her nipples until they were pointy, hard and begging for his mouth to wrap around them. He massaged the insides of her thighs until they began to tremble in the water. Her soft moans grew more frequent while the teasing of her clitoris went from passive to possessive. His fingers played with the folds, tenderly rubbed the swollen bud between his fingers until her entire body began to spasm.

"Spread your legs," he urged.

Jacqueline could barely do as he asked with the thrill of what he was doing to her beat hard and fast. She managed to lift one leg and place it on the side of the tub and then the other, leaving the epicenter of desire wide open and vulnerable. Raymond took immediate advantage, sliding one then two fingers inside the hot cove that pulsed with a life of its own.

She cried out as a burst of pure ecstasy shot through her. She dug her hands into her thighs to keep them open to allow her to continue to receive the pleasure that Raymond was putting on her.

He rained kissed on the back of her neck, along her ear, while one hand kneaded and caressed the swell of her breasts and the other slid in and out her heat.

And then a rushing pulse of water hit her clit when Raymond turned on the jets of the tub. The feeling was electric, shooting through her like a bolt of lighting.

Her entire body jerked in response.

By manipulating the knob, Ray increased and decreased the pulse of water, turning Jacqueline into one solid mass of sensation. His fingers continued to work their magic and the water escalated his efforts.

Hot tears of bliss sprung from the corners of her eyes as her hips instinctively rose and fell to meet the rhythm of the water and the concerto of Raymond's fingers.

The air grew hotter, thicker. The pace rose. Raymond continued to murmur what loving her like this was doing to him. How good she felt. How much he wanted to feel her come before he put himself deep inside of her.

She shook with pleasure when Ray sent that last hot burst of water rushing between her legs and tossed her on a dizzying spiral of inexplicable rapture. Her insides gripped and released with such power that for a moment everything burst into bright lights then went black. Jolts of electricity shot up and down her limbs until she was limp and disconnected from where she was.

Raymond slowly turned off the jets, reducing the pulse by degrees, until it was only his fingers that were giving her pleasure. When he felt the last of her climax subside he extracted his fingers but claimed and calmed her by tenderly covering her hot box with his large hand, soothing it with the gentleness of his touch.

Jacqueline collapsed back against him. Her legs dropped down into the water, splashing them both. She was too weak to laugh.

"Oh. My. God," she finally said on a breath.

Raymond stroked her damp hair away from her face. He kissed the top of her head.

"I have never come like that before in my life."

He grinned. "I know."

She craned her head around so that she could glimpse him and saw the wicked sparkle in his eyes. Playfully, she swatted his arm. "You could have given me a heart attack."

He chuckled. "I seriously doubt that, but what a way to go." He gave her breasts a playful squeeze.

Jacqueline languidly rested against Raymond's chest, lulled by the steady beat of his heart and the soothing warmth of the water. Her body still hummed like a tuning fork that continued to vibrate inside of her. It was a delicious feeling that she didn't want to end. And it wouldn't. While Raymond slowly caressed her breasts she felt his desire grow.

Tantalizingly, she wiggled her hips against him and was rewarded with his ragged moan. He gripped her tighter.

The tub was slippery for what she had in mind but she was willing to try anything once. She lifted the level on the drain and the water began to recede, but before it could empty fully, she turned the water on so that they were only partially in the water as it continued to empty and fill. She turned on the jets and the hot warm water stirred around them.

She turned to straddle him. The water rushed over her clit and she shivered.

In anticipation, Raymond's eyes darkened to almost black. He looped his arms around her waist, lowered his head and pulled a waiting nipple into his mouth. Jacqueline cried out.

She managed to get onto her knees and after a few wiggles and adjustments, lowered herself onto his throbbing member.

The air stuck in her throat. Her eyes widened then squeezed shut as the incredible sensation of him filling her combined with the pressure of the water buoying around them.

The rushing water added to the thrill as it pulsed around and between them, making them work for every thrust, every stroke.

Raymond had held off for as long as he could. His

arms tightened around Jacqueline. The roar of his long-awaited climax seized his calves, jolted up his thighs and erupted in such a powerful burst he hollered in pleasure, thrusting up deep and fast, needing to bury himself inside her. He palmed her firm behind in his large hands and worked her against him until he could feel her insides grip him, sucking out the last of him and sending her on a soaring release that hand her fingers tugging at his hair, her head thrown back in bliss and her body giving way to utter satisfaction.

Jacqueline collapsed against him and dropped her head to his chest.

Their breathing erupted in staccato bursts, tumbling over each other then turning to bubbling laughter at the pure joy that they felt in being together again—really together.

Raymond stoked her hair away from her face and then cupped her cheeks in his hands. His warm gaze moved slowly over her features as if memorizing every detail.

"I love you, J," he whispered and swallowed hard.

Her world shifted.

"There, I said it."

She watched the pulse beat a crazy rhythm at the base of his throat and her own heart was racing so quickly she could barely breathe.

"I fell in love with you in Cairo," she said on a breath and the release, saying the words, was liberating.

Raymond's eyes widened. "What?"

She grinned shyly and nodded.

"You never said anything."

"Neither did you," she countered.

He lifted his chin. "I thought it would make you run."

"It might have," she admitted, knowing how much stock she'd put on her freedom and laying claim to someone emotionally was counter to her mantra. She could have lost him and she would have had no one to blame but herself.

"And now?" Hope hung on those two words.

"I think you're stuck with me."

He pulled her to him and captured her mouth with a searing kiss that left her breathless, aroused and needing him again.

"I love you," she murmured against his lips as he began to caress her again.

"I'm going to show you how much I love you," he said, and then somehow managed to stand with her in his arms and carry her into the adjoining bedroom.

Chapter 14

"When are we leaving for New York?" Raymond spooned closer to Jacqueline. He brushed the hair away from the back of her neck and softly kissed her there.

She craned her head around to get a glimpse of him. "We?"

"Yes. When are *we* leaving for New York?"

She turned away. "*I* plan on leaving day after tomorrow."

He pushed up on his elbow and turned her onto her back so that he could look right at her. "Tomorrow? When were you going to tell me?"

She lowered her gaze, unable to meet the accusation that stared back at her.

"You weren't going to tell me!" He sat up. "Were you planning on leaving me another note?"

She flinched at the sting of his words. "No," she finally said. "I was going to tell you tonight."

He snorted a nasty laugh. "Really." He leaned back against the padded headboard then ran his hands across his face in frustration. "I don't understand you."

She folded her arms beneath her breasts like a petulant child. "You weren't supposed to be here!" she snapped. "You weren't supposed to tell me how you felt about me and screw up my head." She threw her hands up in the hair and sniffed. "Now everything is a mess."

"Oh, so somehow in that crazy, stubborn head of yours this is my fault."

She pressed her lips into a tight, unbreakable line.

Raymond glared at her, completely stunned by her behavior. Then it hit him. Why should he be surprised? *This is Jacqueline Lawson. Jacqueline is always her own woman. She never relies on anyone. Even now when she is scared out of her head.*

He drew in a long sobering breath. "It's okay to be scared." He saw her flinch. "I'm here. And it's okay to let me know that you're scared."

Her gaze skipped up to his, darted away then returned. She slowly shook her head in denial.

"I can only imagine how hard it was growing up in a testosterone-drenched environment where excellence and endurance were demanded, and letting them see you sweat was not an option." He stroked her chin with the tip of his finger. "I know you had to make your own way. And I know much of the time you believed that you were doing it alone so you did everything you could to protect yourself. But, J, you're not like your father. You're not like your brothers. You don't have to be. It's all right to let someone love you and for you to love them back." He paused, taken by the tears that slid down her cheeks. "You're my everything, baby," he said on a ragged breath. "Don't every doubt that. *We* will get through this."

Her shoulders shook and she pressed her face against his chest, letting the sobs of relief drain from her. He held her close, gently rocking her in his arms, uttering soothing sounds into her hair. "I don't know how to do this," she said between her tears.

"We'll do it together. We will." He kissed her cheek.

She sniffed back her tears and wiped her eyes with the knuckle of her finger. Drawing in a deep breath she stole a look at him. "I'm not easy."

"Really?" he teased. "I had no idea."

A laugh bubbled up. "You're right…about my brothers. I never felt that I could compete." She released a long breath. "I was my parent's afterthought."

"That was then."

"I know. Unfortunately it's one of the things that stuck with me over the years." She curled into his arms.

"And it made you into an incredible woman anyway."

She grinned. "I'm going to have to do this damsel

in distress routine more often if I'm going to get this ego boost."

"Anytime, baby. I'll be your knight in shining armor," he said in a really bad British accent.

She playfully nudged him in the ribs. "Don't give up your day job."

They lay together in quiet. The only sound was the light hum of the central air.

"Hey, I have an idea," Raymond said, breaking the tranquil trance that Jacqueline had slipped into.

"Hmm, what's that?"

"Since we only have one good night in the old town, why don't you show me around?"

She sat up a bit and looked at him. "You want to?"

"Yeah. Let's put our stamp on Baton Rouge. You up to it?" he asked, concerned, realizing that she might not have the energy.

"Sure. Okay," she smiled brightly. "Why not? I'll be discovering it with you. It's been a while since I've been back, but the main eating spots are still the same."

"Great." He sat up. He checked his watch. "It's still early. We can hang out for a couple of hours and come back and get a good night's sleep."

Her lashes lowered over her eyes. "Or not," she said, a sly smile curving the corners of her mouth.

"Oh, Ms. Lawson, don't tempt me." He hopped up out of bed and gave her luscious, exposed behind a playful swat. "The clock is ticking."

Jacqueline pulled herself up out of the bed. "I'm

going to take a quick shower…alone," she warned, pointing a finger at him.

He gave her the sad puppy-dog face then quickly brightened. "Hey, no place too fancy. I didn't bring the proper attire." He flashed a crooked grin.

"I have just the place and they have the best beer in Louisiana. Then we can do dinner, listen to some Cajun music…"

"Now you're talking. While you're in the shower, I'll book my flight to New York. What time and what airline?"

She smiled at him from the doorway of the bathroom, her heart filling with love and gratitude. "11:30. Delta."

They drove Raymond's rented Toyota into downtown Baton Rouge and their first stop was Port Royal on College Drive.

"It's not what you call upscale," Jacqueline said as they approached the front door, "but it's fun and relaxing."

"You forget, baby, I'm easily impressed," he joked. He held the door open for her and they stepped inside to the sounds of zydeco.

"Welcome to Port Royal. Would you like a table or do you prefer to sit at the bar?" a young hostess greeted them.

Jacqueline turned to Raymond with a raised brow in question.

"The bar is fine," he said.

The woman extended her hand toward the bar. "Enjoy your evening."

Raymond took Jacqueline's hand and they walked around dancing and bobbing bodies toward the bar and were able to grab two seats near the end.

"What can I get ya?" the bartender asked, while he wiped down the spaces in front of them with a damp white cloth. He plopped a bowl of nuts down on the counter.

"He loves beer. The best," Jacqueline added.

"We have an excellent Austrian beer that you'll love."

"Stiegl?" Raymond asked, sure that they wouldn't have it.

The bartender's eyes widened with delight. "You know your beer. Coming right up. And for you, Miss?"

"I'm having what he's having," she said with a grin, hooking her thumb in Raymond's direction.

Moments later two steins of beer were placed in front of them. "Enjoy."

Raymond bobbed his head in appreciation as he took his first sip. "The real thing," he murmured.

"It is good," Jacqueline agreed, letting the icy cold brew ease down her throat.

Raymond turned to her. "How are you feeling?"

Her expression tightened. "Fine. Why?"

"Just checking, J. Don't get yourself all worked up."

She lifted her glass then put it back down. "Look, one of the reasons why I've kept this illness to myself is because I don't like hovering. I don't want people feeling sorry for me or treating me any differently or asking me every five minutes how I'm feeling."

"I get it, okay? I ask because I care. I ask because I know how you are. You will push yourself to the limits."

She pursed her lips and slowly turned the glass in a slow circle on top of the counter. She pushed out a breath. "Okay, this is how it is. I get tired. Sometimes I get so tired I feel like I can't move. I get light-headed and sometimes I get bouts of nausea. Other times I feel fine. Like today. Like a lot of days." She lowered her head. "I try to eat well, take my meds and rest when I can."

"How could you have kept this from me for so long?" he asked, more hurt than upset.

She shrugged a shoulder. "It wasn't easy." She took a swallow of her beer. "Especially when I wasn't feeling well."

"I knew something was wrong. For a while I knew something was wrong. You weren't yourself—toward me."

"I know. And I'm sorry. I...I thought if I put up a wall, put some distance between us emotionally...and physically, that leaving would be easier."

He turned on his stool so that he could look directly at her. "Was it?"

She shook her head. "No. It was the hardest thing I've ever had to do."

Raymond covered her hand with his. "I'm really glad you said that. If you told me it was easy..."

She lifted his hand and pressed her lips against his knuckles. "I'm glad you came. I really am," she admitted.

"Me, too."

"How's the beer?" the bartender asked, interrupting their moment.

"Excellent." Raymond raised his glass to him. "Great suggestion."

"You folks let me know if you need anything else."

"Thanks," Jacqueline said.

Raymond took a look around. "Pretty nice place and you were right about the beer."

"Told ya. Let me know when you get hungry and we can get going to the restaurant."

"Ready when you are."

They finished off their beers, paid the tab and headed out.

"Things are kind of spread out in Baton Rouge, not like New Orleans. But we have our share of nightspots. Make the next left," she directed. "And no matter where you go in Louisiana, the food is really phenomenal."

"I've been to NOLA for Mardi Gras about fifteen years ago. Now *that* was a wild experience," he said, laughter filling his voice.

"Yeah, it gets all kinds of crazy out there. It's on the next street on your right."

Raymond eased the car onto the tight street and lucked out on a parking space. He got out and helped

Jacqueline from the car. He looped his arm around her waist and they walked inside.

The cool dim interior was dotted with tables and booths, a dance floor and small stage with a four-piece jazz band was playing.

"Good evening. Do you have a reservation?" a model-perfect hostess asked. Her all-black attire hugged her slender figure.

"No, we don't have reservations," Jacqueline said. "But we'd like a table for two."

"Sure. The wait will be about twenty minutes."

"No problem. We can wait," Raymond said, bobbing his head to the music.

"There's a lounge upstairs and a small bar."

"Great."

"Can I have your name?"

"Jordan," Raymond said.

"Someone will call you when your table is ready."

Raymond took Jacqueline's hand and they walked upstairs. The upper lounge was as crowded as the main floor.

"Busy place," Raymond commented, looking over heads for a seat.

"It will be worth the wait," Jacqueline assured.

They walked around couples and groups of night-clubbers.

"Isn't that your nephew over there?" Raymond asked, lifting his chin in the direction of a small group.

Jacqueline followed Raymond's gaze and settled on

her nephew. Rafe was in a lively conversation at the bar with two women. As always, he was effortlessly charming, dividing his attention between the two lovelies.

Jacqueline and Raymond walked over.

"Rafe. . ."

He glanced over his shoulder and his face lit up. He got up from the cushioned bar stool. "Aunt J." He kissed her cheek. "Ray, right?" He stuck out his hand, which Raymond shook.

"What are you doing here? Are you okay? I mean…"

Jacqueline smiled. "I'm feeling pretty good. I wanted to show Raymond around. We're waiting on a table for dinner."

"Excuse my bad manners. Cherise, Linda this is my fabulous aunt Jacquie." Jacqueline blushed. "And her friend Ray."

"Nice to meet you," they said in unison.

"Hey, listen, no need to wait for a table. I have one reserved right up front. You can sit there."

"I don't want to impose on you and your friends," Jacqueline said.

"No imposition. It's for me and the guys in the band."

"The band?"

He grinned. "Yeah, I forget you've been away for a while. I play with a band. Sax. Much to my father's great dismay," he added with a sly grin.

"I can imagine," Jacqueline said, a tinge of sarcasm in her tone. "Sure. If it's okay with the band." She looked to Raymond for confirmation.

"Cool with me," Ray said.

"Great. I'll let Yvette know."

"Yvette?"

"The hostess."

"How long have you been playing here?"

"Hmm, usually one weekend a month. Guess you lucked out. It's my one weekend." He lifted his glass of bourbon from the bar. "Ladies, as always it was a pleasure." He buzzed both of their cheeks then led the way back downstairs. He found Yvette, who quickly got Jacqueline and Raymond settled at the table where two of Rafe's band members were seated before their set.

"Mike, Percy, this is my aunt Jacqueline. So watch your mouths," he joked. "And her friend Ray Jordan."

Ray shook hands with the men while Jacqueline nodded in greeting. He helped her into her seat.

"Whatever you want is on the house," Yvette said.

Jacqueline's brows rose. "Oh." She stole a quick look at Rafe who winked at her. "Thank you."

"Can I get you a drink?" She looked from one to the other.

"I'll take a white wine spritzer," Jacqueline said.

"What are you drinking, Rafe?" Raymond asked.

"I'm a straight bourbon man."

"Bourbon sounds good," he said to Yvette.

"I'll have your waitress bring them right over." She gave Rafe a secret smile as she departed and he followed her every move then turned back to the gathering at the table.

"The crawfish is the best in the city," Rafe said.

"I remember," Jacqueline said, picking up her menu. "And the étouffée." Her eyes rolled to the top of her head in delight.

Mike and Percy chuckled.

"I'm game. I haven't had an authentic Cajun meal in ages," Raymond said.

"You won't be disappointed."

"Fellas, we need to get set up," Rafe said as he rose from his seat. His band members followed suit.

"Nice meeting you both," Mike said.

"Enjoy the show," Percy added.

"That was a surprise," Jacqueline said, once they were gone.

"You mean about Rafe?"

She nodded. "I mean I knew he fooled around with music but I had no idea that he was doing it semi-professionally. Branford must have nightmares at night about it." She sipped her drink.

"Why?"

Jacqueline's brows knitted for a bit. "Rafe was supposed to be the heir apparent to the Lawson political throne. Since Rafe was a kid, whatever Branford wanted him to do, he did the opposite. It would infuriate him. When he got into his teens he became even more rebellious. He chose his own path. I think in a strange way as much as my brother railed against Rafe's behavior, he grudgingly admires his son for standing up to him."

Raymond studied her over the rim of her glass,

mildly amused at her take on her nephew. "Sounds a lot like you."

Her gaze jumped to his. Her mouth pinched into a smile. "Guess that's why we always got along. Kindred spirits."

"Ready to order?" their waitress asked, appearing at their side.

"You do the honors," Raymond said.

Jacqueline ordered the étouffée and a side of crawfish, just as the MC announced the next set.

The houselights dimmed and the spotlight shone down on the assembled band, with Rafe up front. They launched into their rendition of Grover Washington Jr.'s "Mr. Magic."

"He's good," Raymond said, tapping his foot to the familiar rhythm.

Jacqueline grinned with pride. Then they segued to John Coltrane's "My Favorite Things," followed by Coleman Hawkins' "Indian Summer" and wrapped it up with Coltrane's "Love Supreme," to the roar of the crowd.

Raymond was on his feet like much of the crowd when the set came to its rousing conclusion.

"Wow, that brother can blow," he said, taking his seat.

"I had no idea," Jacqueline said, awed by her nephew's prowess on the soprano sax.

Moments later the trio made their way through the crowd, stopping along the way to shake hands, accept back slaps and accolades. They split up halfway to the table and it was Rafe who joined Jacqueline and Raymond.

Raymond stood halfway and greeted him. "Awesome job, man."

"We try," Rafe said, sitting down then leaning back in his chair, still hyped by his performance.

Jacqueline leaned over and covered his hand. "Fabulous," she said on a breath. Her eyes glowed.

"Thanks. Means a lot coming from you, Aunt J."

"Do you only play in Louisiana?" Raymond asked.

"Mostly in New Orleans. We've had some offers to come up to the jazz clubs in New York. I played in Paris last spring." He shrugged nonchalantly. "Things are opening up. But New Orleans is still the home of jazz."

"You ever think about recording?"

"Hmm, I've been asked." He shook his head. "Not really interested in getting all tied up with someone else's demands and time schedules. I don't want this to become a job."

Jacqueline bit back a smile and wondered if he'd feel the same way if he didn't have the Lawson money behind him.

The waiter brought their meal and asked what Rafe wanted. He ordered another bourbon and decided to nibble on the crawfish.

"So, Aunt J." His eyes darted to Raymond for a minute then back to his aunt. "Have you changed your mind?"

Chapter 15

The mood at the table shifted.

Jacqueline looked down at her plate. "No. We're leaving for New York day after tomorrow."

Rafe studied her for a moment. "You plan on seeing the family before you go?"

"I'll call Dom and Justin. I'm seeing *you* now." She forced a smile. "Lee Ann is back in D.C. and Desi is on her honeymoon."

"So you really aren't going to see my father?"

"No. There's no reason to see Branford. He made it clear when he saw me at the wedding that I wasn't welcome."

Raymond took a mouthful of food, chewed slowly before he spoke. "She's stubborn."

She threw him a look that he ignored.

"Family trait," Rafe quipped.

"I'm not going to sit here and have the two of you gang up on me."

"Never let it be said that I ganged up on a lady." Rafe winked and slowly stood. "Take good care of her," he said to Raymond.

"I intend to." He stood up and shook Rafe's hand with both of his. "Thanks, man," he said quietly.

"Let me know how she's doing."

"I will."

Rafe rounded the table and leaned down to kiss his aunt's cheek. "Call me…or something."

She smiled up at him. "I will. Thank you for everything, Rafe. I don't know what I would have done if you hadn't been there."

"Don't stay away so long next time."

She squeezed his hand before he turned and walked away.

"Can I get you anything else?" their waiter asked.

"No, I think we're good," Raymond said, "unless you want something else, J."

"No. Thanks."

"I hope you enjoyed your meal. Please come again."

The busboy appeared and began taking their plates.

"Let's walk off this food," Jacqueline suggested.

"Sure."

Once outside it was a typical Louisiana night. A warm breeze blew in from the Mississippi leaving the air muggy, the skin slightly damp and hair curling up at the back of your neck.

The sky was incredibly clear and the sound of music and the scent of food were part of the nightlife.

"I was always intrigued by the mystique of Louisiana," Raymond said. He held Jacqueline's hand then tucked it in the curve of his arm. "The stories of the bayou, the houses of ill repute." He laughed. "The food, of course the music, and the twist of the language."

"Hmm, you forgot vampires."

He tossed his head back and laughed. "Right." He turned to look at her. "What were you like as a young girl?"

She half smiled. "Willful, kind of tom-boyish when I was younger." She followed the shadow of her footsteps as they walked. "I guess I wanted to be the boy that my father wanted. I had a few good friends. I enjoyed school. I was supposed to get a degree in global finance, which would have thrilled my father to no end." She shrugged slightly.

"Global finance. You're kidding?"

"Nope."

"How did you make the switch to photography?"

She drew in a long breath and thought back to that night of her father's win in the general election. The house was full of supporters. Champagne was flowing. Raucous laughter filled the air. Her brothers were in their element, glad-handing and schmoozing with the political and financial powerbrokers. Jacqueline may as well have been yesterday's lunch for all the attention that was paid to her. She decided to occupy herself with the present her mother had given her a few years earlier—a Nikon camera.

She'd only used it a few times but after a couple of missteps she got the hang of it, and began snapping pictures of the festivities. It must have been nearly a month later when she thought about the camera again and went to have the film developed.

"I know I shouldn't be commenting on customers' photographs," the clerk had said to her, "but did you take these photos?"

"Yes, why? Is there a problem?"

"No, not at all. These are really good. I mean really good."

Jacqueline was so completely taken aback she didn't know what to think. "And you know this how?"

"In my other life, I do freelance photography for a couple of magazines and they are always looking for people. You'd be perfect."

Her interest was piqued. "Are you serious?"

"Very serious. You're really good. The composition is fantastic. The lighting." He looked right at her. "You have talent."

Jacqueline smiled at the memory. "His name was Peter Jennings. He gave me the 'shutterbug.' Got me my first assignment, mentored me and let me cry on his shoulder when my father went ballistic when I decided to drop out of LSU and take up photography."

"Hmm, that must have been rough."

"To a point. After all the yelling and gnashing of teeth," she snickered, "and threats to be tossed out of the family will, I knew what I was going to do and it didn't matter what my father and my brothers said or thought. I never respond well to yelling and threats." She glanced at him from beneath her lashes to see his amused smile.

"And the rest is history as they say," Raymond said.

"Sort of. I went to New York. Studied, met Traci and slowly started building a reputation for myself."

"I'm still amazed that you were able to keep the Lawson name from sticking to you all these years."

"There are two people—not including you—who know who my brother is, but I made it clear I would never trade in my name for a story or a photograph. I want what I do to be of my own merit. I don't want special treatment or be expected to do more than anyone else."

Raymond stopped walking. He clasped her shoulders and looked down into her eyes, lit by the overhead streetlights. The unique music of cicadas teased the air that was perfumed with the scents of magnolia blossoms and jasmine.

"And it's one of the many things that I love about you," he began, "your determination to be your own woman." He paused a beat. "I know you don't want to hear this, but I'm going to say it. I think your stubbornness, your unwillingness to break this invisible code that you have is going to be to your detriment…or ours."

She turned away. "I've made up my mind, Ray. And if you can't deal with it then…"

"Then what, J? What? You'll run off again?"

Her eyes snapped. She turned on her heel and headed back to where the car was parked.

"Is this going to be your answer to everything that you don't want to deal with?" he demanded, catching up with her.

She stopped in midstep. The heat from her eyes was gone, replaced with a barely dim light. "Let's not do this, Ray." Her eyes moved slowly over his. "This is what I was trying to avoid."

He lowered his head for a moment then looked at her. "If I didn't love you, J, I wouldn't give a damn what you did or how you did it. But I do and that means I'm invested in this thing and I'm not always going to say what you want me to say, but I'm going to say what's on my mind and in my heart. And if I'm going to have to deal with your pigheadedness, you'll have to deal with mine."

Her mouth tightened then quivered ever so slightly at the corners as a smile teased her. "Deal," she finally agreed.

Raymond's dark gaze lightened. He slowly lowered his head and touched his mouth to hers before wrapping his arms tightly around her and molding her to his body. The thought of not having her terrified him in a way that explosions, car bombs and government coups or being lost in African jungles and desert wastelands never had.

The simple kiss mushroomed as their lips and tongues toyed with each other, eliciting soft sighs and rough groans.

"Let's go home," she whispered against his mouth.

"Let's."

Back at the hotel, the hunger that was fueled between them on the car ride home, with the slight touches on a thigh, fingers stroking a knee, a look, a sigh, all ballooned and exploded the moment they crossed the threshold.

All Raymond could think about was to possess her and make her understand that she was his and he was hers. To him that meant opening yourself, baring that part of your soul that no one else was allowed to see. It meant good and bad times. Yet, even as he stripped her bare and her lush honey-toned body was stretched out before him, he knew that possessing Jacqueline Lawson was like trying to hold the wind in your hand. You could feel it but when you opened your fist there was nothing left but the sensation.

But at least for now, for these moments when he moved in and out of the hot wet passage to her soul and she raised her hips to meet his every thrust and her legs rode up his back in wild abandon, and her cries of pleasure and the strangled calls of his name lit a fire in his belly—she was his.

The next day Jacqueline and Ray spent the morning touring New Orleans, taking pictures and sampling all the New Orleans delicacies. They even took a boat ride along the Mississippi.

By the time they returned to the hotel, Jacqueline was beyond exhausted. Her limbs felt like they would give out on her at any minute. Tiny dark spots danced in front of her eyes and her skin was clammy to the touch.

Raymond asked her several times if she was feeling all right as she'd grown quiet as the day progressed. But she insisted that she was fine.

She needed to lie down and close her eyes so that Raymond wouldn't get to glimpse the fear that rested there. She'd only been out of the hospital a couple of days. She'd even had a transfusion. She was taking her meds. She was eating well. Yet, she was feeling the way she did before she collapsed. It was much too soon to have sunk this far so quickly. Something was wrong.

"I'm going to take a shower and lie down. I'm really tired," she said, not daring to look at him.

"Are you sure you're all right?" He walked over to her. She turned to get her robe from the foot of the bed.

"Look at me."

She barely glanced up.

He clasped her shoulder to cease her movements.

"Look at me." She rolled her eyes, glanced up and stared at him.

"Happy now?"

"No. Not really. Your skin is cold."

"I told you, I'm tired!" she snapped, more forceful than necessary.

He released her and held up his hands in submission. "Fine." He backed up. "You're tired. You need a shower. Fine." He turned and walked out into the front of the suite.

She was so weak her insides quivered. This is what she didn't want—Raymond hovering over her, seeing her vulnerable and wanting to make things better. Didn't he realize that he couldn't?

She struggled to get out of her clothes. It felt as if it was taking forever and her clothing weighed a ton. She didn't want to risk falling in the shower, so she ran the tub water and sat in the tub while it filled.

What if the experimental treatments didn't work? The question continued to haunt her. Each time that it crossed her thoughts her pulse would race out of control and the bubbling feeling of dread rose from the balls of her feet all the way up to her throat. Even as she touted all the new developments, what she didn't reveal was that with the advanced stage of her illness, the chances of the treatment working were greatly diminished.

Tears spilled from her eyes and her slender body shook as she wept, muffling the sounds by pressing her fist to her mouth. She rested her chin on her bent knees and wrapped her arm around her legs. Oh, God, what if it didn't work? She didn't want Raymond to be there to hear it or see it in her eyes. She couldn't bear it. She simply couldn't.

It had to work. It had to.

Chapter 16

Jacqueline sat on the side of the bed, sticking her feet into her slip-on shoes, better for getting out of at airport security, and talking to Traci on her cell phone that was tucked between her shoulder and her ear.

"Yes, I forgive you. I know you were only thinking of me."

"Once you get settled in New York, I'll be out to see you. I still can't imagine you not being here," Traci said, the strains of melancholy filtering through her voice.

"I know. I'll have to see how things work out. At the time I thought it was the right decision to pack it all up and move to New York."

"But…"

She sighed. "I'm not sure about much of anything

right now. I only want to get through these treatments and then make some decisions."

"Well, you know in this market your condo may take a while to sell."

"Actually, I didn't put it on the market."

"What?"

"Nope."

"In case you wanted to come back," Traci stated more than asked.

"Yeah."

"Ready?" Raymond called out from the front room. "The car is here."

"Listen, sweetie, I gotta go. I'll call you as soon as I can when we get to New York."

"Let Ray take care of you for once and do what the doctors say."

"Yes, ma'am. I'll certainly try."

"Love you."

"Love you back."

Jacqueline tucked her phone in her purse, quickly checked the room for any forgotten items then joined Raymond at the front door. The bellhop put their bags on the luggage cart and they headed out. In about five hours they would be at her rented apartment on West 72nd Street, blocks away from New York Presbyterian/Weill Cornell Medical Center where some of the most innovative medical discoveries were happening every day.

She was feeling better than she had the previous evening. She'd slept soundly, curled in Ray's embrace. The solid, steady beat of his heart soothed her throughout the night and she awoke renewed and much more like herself. Her limbs didn't feel as if they'd been shot with lead. Her thoughts were clear and the spots were gone. What if all that it took to cure her was a good night's sleep in the arms of a man who loved her?

"What's that secret smile?" Raymond softly asked as he settled back into his seat and fastened his belt.

"If I told you it wouldn't be a secret."

"Ah, touché. Anything that makes you smile is fine with me." He reached over and held her hand for the rest of the flight.

They landed nearly an hour behind schedule at New York's JFK Airport due to raging thunderstorms that had sprung up along the East Coast. The temperature was in the eighties and if it was possible the humidity was higher than in Baton Rouge.

There was no mistaking that they were in New York. The moment they stepped out of the terminal to get in line for a cab, the electric energy of the "city that never sleeps" was palpable. Everything and everyone moved faster, talked faster and seemed to enjoy life at a faster pace. There was an intangible excitement that seeped into the air that was breathed as if all the inhabitants on the isle of Manhattan were secretly being shot with tiny jolts of electricity.

Jacqueline had been all around the world and back

again and next to her home in L.A. and her roots in Baton Rouge, New York was her favorite city.

The yellow cab zipped along the highway, swerved around cars that were moving too slowly and in no time flat the cabbie was zooming to a stop in front of Jacqueline's building.

"I'd forgotten how crazy the New York cabbies were," Raymond said under his breath. Jacqueline giggled.

Raymond grabbed their bags from the trunk, paid the driver, and before they could put two feet in front of them, the cabbie had sped away. They looked at each other and shook their heads in amusement.

Jacqueline looked up at the three-story brownstone. *Her new home.* She fished in her purse for the keys that had been mailed to her by the NY realtor. She tugged in a deep breath, stole a quick look at Raymond then took her first steps toward her new abode.

Her fingers shook ever so slightly as she slipped the key in the lock of the wrought-iron gate on the ground level. Raymond locked the door behind them and they walked into a small foyer that was already adorned with her small side table and topped with a vase filled with spring flowers. The mahogany woodwork gleamed and the hardwood floors sparkled as if they'd been hand polished. Her black-and-white photo of John Coltrane hung on the wall above the table and vase.

The anxiety that she felt diminished a bit after seeing the touch of home. If the entryway was any indication of the work that the designer and movers had done, then much of her anxiety would be alleviated. All she'd seen were pictures and had a virtual tour but this was the real thing.

To their left were wide mahogany sliding doors that, if memory served her, opened onto the enormous living room, then dining room and a kitchen.

Jacqueline pulled the doors open and her breath caught. The room belonged in a magazine. The centerpiece of the room was the massive brick fireplace and mantel, above which soared a massive mirror, framed in wood and brick that rose to the height of the cathedral ceiling. The all-white furniture—six-foot couch, love seat and two armchairs—were strategically placed throughout the room. Low glass-and-wood coffee tables braced the seating. Teal and soft orange were the accents for the room—from overstuffed pillows to throws to the casual oval rug. Along the back wall next to the archway that led to the dining room was a built-in bar. And from what Jacqueline could see, it was fully stocked. More of her photographs graced the walls.

They walked through to the dining area that was decorated with a long, slender table that would easily seat twelve. A rectangular-shaped chandelier that resembled a waterfall hung over the center of the table. Beyond the dining room was the kitchen that was the size of many apartments. White cabinets above and below provided ample storage and the stainless steel appliances gleamed. A center island with a built-in sink and wok still had enough room for seating of six.

Jacqueline walked over to the window and peeked out at the garden that had been expertly tended from what she could tell.

She spun toward Raymond wide-eyed and with a smile blooming on her face. "This place is…incredible," she said on a breath and giggled with delight.

Raymond nodded but didn't comment. He ran his hand along the granite counter.

"Come on let's go upstairs," she urged, with child-like excitement in her voice. She grabbed his hand and tugged him behind her back down the hallway and up the wide, winding staircase to the floor above.

The long hallway also had wide sliding doors to the right of the top of the staircase along with a door that led back out front.

Raymond did the honors and opened the sliding doors to reveal an intimate sitting- and reading room. A wide wooden desk that Raymond recognized from the apartment in L.A., sat beneath the floor-to-ceiling windows that were topped off with stained glass. Tucked in the built-ins along the side of the desk was some of Jacqueline's camera equipment.

The center of the sprawling room used yet another fireplace as the focal point with two matching uphol-stered armchairs in a vibrant print of cherry-red, yellows and greens, and an antique chair with the seat cushion in a bold white-and-gold stripe. Two three-legged tables finished off the sitting area. At the far end of the room, built-in bookcases were lined with many of the photography books that she'd shipped ahead, along with an assortment of classic lit and noir fiction.

Jacqueline strolled along the hardwood floors and pulled open the frosted French doors that revealed her bedroom. It was exactly the way she'd described it to the designer. The king-size bed faced the bay window that looked out onto the garden. The bed was covered in a brilliant winter-white comforter that looked to be five inches thick. Dozens of pillows in a multitude of colors, shapes and sizes were on top. At the foot of the bed was a large oak chest. Mounted above the short headboard, encased in a black frame, was the official attire of a Japanese geisha that she'd purchased on one of her trips.

Vases overflowing with flowers sat on top of the dresser, the nightstand and in the window. She was thrilled to find that her clothes had been unpacked and hung up.

She spun toward Raymond, pure delight on her face and stopped cold when she saw his thunderous expression. "What's wrong?"

His jaw clenched. His eyes scorched every surface then fell back on her. "Just how long were you planning this? Weeks, months?" His voice held a deathly calm, just above a harsh whisper. "This wasn't some spur-of-the-moment thing." He ran his hand across his head in frustration. He took a step toward her and stopped.

"Look at this place." His chest heaved in and out as he stretched his arms. "You were really going to leave. Just like that." He snapped his fingers and she flinched as if a shot had been fired. "Without one damn word and without looking back! You had a whole other life set up and ready to go." His scowl was so deep it cut a groove between his eyes.

Jacqueline squared her shoulders and lifted her chin. "You're right. I hired a Realtor, a moving company and a designer—three months ago. I'd planned to leave and not come back." She watched the muscles of his throat work but he didn't speak. He simply stared at her as if seeing her through a mist. Her heart thundered in her chest. She felt the sting in her eyes but she would not cry as she watched him pick up his bag, turn without a word and walk out.

Chapter 17

Raymond stalked out of the apartment. His temples pounded. He had no idea where he was going or what he was going to do next. All he was certain of was that he had to get away before he truly said something that he would regret and could never take back.

He walked along 72nd Street, hurt and anger blurring his vision. For the first time in their often-tumultuous relationship, he had no idea who Jacqueline Lawson really was. That realization gouged a hole in his gut. He'd been in love with her for years. Although unspoken until recently, he was sure that she never doubted that he cared deeply for her and would do anything within his power to keep her happy and safe. Declaring his love for her, to Jacqueline, was akin to staking a claim, and she was not one to be nailed down or possessed in any way. So he'd kept those three powerful words to himself, only declaring them because he honestly felt that they were well beyond the superficial boundaries that had been established. He'd wanted to reassure her that no matter what, he was there for her. That's what you did for someone that you loved.

But now, he had no idea who that someone was. How could she have been so secretive and deceitful for so many months? She looked him in the eyes day after day, made love with him, shared her life with him and never revealed what her plans were. What kind of woman did that? What else didn't he know about her and may never know? Is that the kind of relationship that he wanted— one filled with secrets and personal agendas?

He wasn't sure what feeling was worst, the anger or the sense of betrayal.

Continuing along 72nd Street, he came upon Sambuca, an upscale restaurant. He stopped momentarily, tempted to go, in but decided it was a place for a date and not for a man who needed to be alone with a stiff drink.

He hoisted the strap of his carry-on higher up on his shoulder and kept walking. He turned onto Amsterdam Avenue and saw the Sugar Bar up ahead. He remembered that Valerie Simpson and her late husband Nick Ashford owned the restaurant. He pulled open the door and stepped inside.

The deep dark woods, warm reds and vibrant oranges were like a welcoming embrace. African art and artifacts graced the walls. Soft music played somewhere in the background.

It was smaller than he'd thought, but that gave the space an intimate vibe. He walked over to the wrap-around bar and slid onto a stool.

"Hi, what can I get for you?" the female bartender asked.

Today he would forgo his usual brew. He needed something stronger.

"Bourbon."

"We have Jim Beam black label and white label. Or would you prefer something else?"

"Black label. Thanks."

She placed a shot glass in front of him and poured the amber liquid to the rim. "Would you like anything from the menu?"

"Sure, let me take a look."

She took a menu from beneath the counter and placed it in front of him.

He glanced at the name tag pinned to her chest. "Thanks, Denise."

She gave him a smile that lasted a bit longer than necessary before turning to the next customer.

Ray opened the menu and scanned the selections, just as his cell phone rang. He pulled it from his pocket half hoping that it would be Jacqueline ready with some kind of explanation that made sense. It was his friend Matt.

"Hey, Matt…"

"Hey, bro. What's up? You back in L.A.?"

"Naw. A change of plans." He lifted his drink and took a swallow. The warm burn filled his belly.

"What kind of change?"

Ray heard water running in the background. "Detour to New York. Long story."

"New York? What the…you're here in the city and you didn't call a brother?"

"Huh?" Then it hit him. Matt had headed to New York after their assignment in Indonesia. So much had happened in the last week, he'd totally forgotten.

"Sorry, man. Happened kinda fast."

"Where are you staying?"

His gut shifted. Visions of Jacqueline's apartment flashed in his head. "At the moment, the Sugar Bar."

"You're staying at the Sugar Bar?" He chuckled, believing Ray was joking. "No, seriously, where are you staying? We can get together while you're in town. Is J with you?"

"Naw." He took another swallow and it went to his head.

"Naw, we can't get together or naw J's not with you?"

"J's not with me." He finished off his drink and singled Denise for another.

Matt was quiet for a moment. "I'm just about finished what I was doing." The sound of running water ceased. "Why don't I meet you over there in about twenty minutes? We can toss back a few."

Ray gave a ragged laugh. "I'm way ahead of you

on that one, bro." Denise put his second drink down in front of him.

"Don't get too far ahead. I won't be able to catch up. See you in a few."

"Yeah. In a few." He disconnected the call then looked at his phone wondering if he may have missed a call or text from Jacqueline. Nothing. He took a long swallow from his drink. Matt better get there pretty quick.

By the time Matt Davis arrived at the Sugar Bar, Ray was seated at a table and on his fourth bourbon. Life was getting fuzzy around the edges.

Matt slid onto the chair opposite him. Raymond glanced up through eyes that were beginning to glaze.

"Good stuff," he said, lifting his glass to Matt.

Matt grabbed Raymond by the wrist to hold the ascent of the glass to his mouth. "How many is this one?" he asked, keeping his tone light.

"Hmm. Don't know."

"Let's get some food to soak up all this good bourbon." He signaled for the waitress.

"We'll take two steak dinners, baked potato and collard greens," Matt said to the waitress. He refocused his attention on his friend. "You wanna tell me what's going on, man?"

Raymond blinked Matt into focus. "Betrayal is kinda f'd up, ya know."

"Sounds like a blues lyric."

Raymond stared into the bottom of his glass. The corner of his mouth curled into more of a snarl than a grin. "Yeah."

"What's going on, man? What happened with you and Jacqueline?"

"Lied to me…for months. Planned on leaving me," he muttered.

"What? What are you talking about? J?" he asked in disbelief. He figured it was the bourbon talking but a part of him knew better. Raymond didn't get wasted. He liked to stay on point. Something definitely happened. But he didn't think Raymond was in the frame of mind to explain. Instead Matt made small talk until their food arrived.

By the time they'd finished their meal, Raymond had sobered up enough so that he didn't sound as if he was talking in slow motion. What Matt was able to get out of him was something about Jacqueline being really ill and she'd come to New York for some kind of special treatment and he'd left her because he didn't know her anymore.

It didn't make sense to him even if it made sense to Raymond. What Matt did know for sure was that Raymond had no place to stay.

Matt paid the tab and they headed to his condo on 56th Street.

Raymond flopped down on the couch and stretched his long legs out in front of him. He leaned his head back against the couch cushion and closed his eyes. At least nothing was spinning, he thought absently.

The aroma of fresh brewed coffee wafted under his nose. He stirred and lazily opened his eyes. Matt was standing above him with a mug of coffee in his hand.

"Thanks." Raymond took the mug. "Did I fall asleep?"

"Yeah, for about an hour. How are you feeling?"

"Better." He took a sip of the steaming coffee.

Matt took a seat opposite him in an armchair. "You feel like talking about it?"

Raymond exhaled a long, slow breath. "I don't understand how she could do something like that. I mean, okay, I got over her pulling up stakes. I went for her reason that she didn't want to be a burden. But…when we got to New York and I saw where she'd set up her new place, it hit me. She'd been planning all this behind my back for months. I was sleeping with this woman, man, and she was doing all this right under my nose. Feel like a real sucker." He said the last word like it was a contagious disease.

Matt rolled over in his head what he'd heard. What could he say? Sometimes people did real dumb mess, especially to people that they care about, maybe *because* they care.

"I'm not going to tell you what to do. You know what you want. I will say that, regardless of how pissed off you might be, this is the time to put your feelings aside and be there for her. She screwed up. She should have been up-front with you. But you know the deal now. You know why she did it. You don't have to agree with it. But you gotta give it to her. Jacqueline is her own woman. It's what you love about her. You've told me so yourself." He paused, waiting for his words to sink in. "She thought she was sparing you."

Raymond's eyes settled on his friend then glanced away. "Yeah, maybe," he conceded.

"The couch pulls out," Matt said as he stood. "I'll get you some sheets."

Chapter 18

Jacqueline was the cat on a hot tin roof. She jumped at every creak of a floorboard, distant voice and blare of car horns. She couldn't count the number of times she'd paced to the front window, pulled back the curtain and peered up and down the unfamiliar streets hoping to see Raymond.

She'd picked up her phone and dialed his number a half-dozen times but disconnected the call before it rang. What could she say? She didn't know where to begin. She'd deceived him. Had she been on trial she would surely be convicted of premeditated betrayal.

She dragged one of the club chairs up to the window that faced the street, settled down, pulled her knees up to her chest and waited. He had to come back. But what would she do if he didn't?

Something startled her. She jumped and her body screamed from the pretzel-like position it had been held in for hours. The rattling of a garbage truck began to fade into the distance. She blinked against the rose-colored light that hung above the skyline of Manhattan. She rubbed her eyes and unwrapped her body. Her limbs protested as she slowly stood.

She'd fallen asleep in the chair. Her heart suddenly pounded as her thoughts cleared. *Ray.* She fumbled on the windowsill for her phone and snatched it up, certain that she'd missed his call.

Nothing.

Her spirits sank. She wandered downstairs to the kitchen and put on a pot of coffee.

Staring into the dark brew she weighed her options. She could simply go on with her plans. Pray that the treatments worked and move on with her life, however it turned out—alone. Or she could pick up her phone, call Ray and ask his forgiveness and tell him that she couldn't do this without him. She didn't want to do this without him.

She gripped her coffee cup. She'd spent her entire life beating odds, defying expectations from her family and her colleagues. But it came with a price. She had to keep everyone at a distance in order to maintain the facade that she'd created.

A tear plopped into her mug of coffee. She didn't want to do it alone anymore.

She picked up her cell phone and this time she let it ring.

"I'm sorry," she said the instant that the call connected. The seconds ticked away with no response. She felt as if the surf was pounding in her ears. "Ray... please talk to me."

"I don't plan on spending any more days or nights without you, J. You either let me in for the long haul or we part ways now. It's up to you."

She squeezed her eyes shut, fought against the instincts that she'd guarded with all of her being. "I want you in it for the long haul."

"I'll be there in twenty minutes." He disconnected the call.

When Raymond pulled up in a cab twenty minutes later, Jacqueline was waiting for him on the stoop, with the forlorn look of the last child to be picked up after school. He'd never felt such a surge of relief and happiness. He paid the driver.

Jacqueline stood as he approached and flung herself against his chest. His arms wrapped around her and lifted her off her feet. His mouth covered hers in a searing kiss that tingled all the way down to her toes.

"I'm sorry. I'm so sorry," she murmured against his mouth. Her heart pounded like crazy in her chest.

"It's going to be all right, baby," he said, kissing her

cheeks, her throat. He ran his fingers through her hair. "It's going to be all right," he repeated. Slowly he lowered her to her feet.

Jacqueline looked up into his eyes and saw the truth of his words reflected there. She believed him because she needed to believe him if she was going to get through this. She took his hand and led him inside.

They wasted no time in reconnecting. They went at each other with a kind of hunger that would not easily be satisfied.

Raymond paid homage to every inch of Jacqueline's body starting at her ankles. His tiny kisses along the slender bones and sensitive skin sent shivers running up her legs. He slowly and methodically worked his way up, stroking and laving until her blood was on fire. Her insides fluttered like the wings of a bird and when his hot kisses met the back of her knees and the insides of her thighs, bright hot white lights exploded behind her lids.

Her moans were music to his ears. He wanted to conquer her body and soul. He wanted her to let go, really let go and give herself to him—commit.

He parted her thighs and in maddeningly slow degrees he reached her epicenter. He teased, he nibbled, he tenderly suckled her until her cries rose to the cathedral ceilings and wrapped around them in an erotic burst that made her body buck and whine. Her head thrashed back and forth on the thick downy pillow as she gripped the sheets in her fists. She called out to the heavens, but it was Ray who answered her.

He answered her with every caress, every kiss, every whisper of her name. He answered her as he slowly entered her, stopping the air from reaching her lungs. He answered her when he moved deeper and deeper inside and then remained perfectly, crazily still while he filled her. He answered her when he began to move inside her, urging her with each thrust of his hips to join him on this inexplicable ride of pleasure.

And she did. Her pelvis rose hard against him. Her thighs tightened around his waist, binding him tightly to her. She offered up the fruit of her breasts that he feasted on while he cupped the globes of her behind and buried his length to the hilt.

Jacqueline bucked and wound her hips when the pulse began deep in her belly. It was that electric flurry that skims the skin and short-circuits the nerves then erupts in a cascade of pure pleasure. She wrapped her arms and legs around him as he drove into her faster and harder, his own climax seconds away. His raw growl of release set her off again and their union exploded in a barrage of unmitigated bliss.

They remained entwined together, their breathing pantlike as they slowly recovered, cooing and stroking each other.

Raymond kissed the top of her damp forehead. "Today is a new day, baby. For both of us."

She nodded her head in agreement against his chest.

"That means you have really got to trust me and I've got to remember to give you the space that you need—even when I don't like it."

She bit back a giggle and then peeked up at him. "We have to deal with the treatment my way," she said, all humor gone from her eyes. "I can't handle it any other way."

"Sometimes you don't know what's best for you," he countered.

"Maybe not, but I have to do this my way. Promise me."

He heaved a long, deep breath. "All right. Your way."

Her taut muscles relaxed. "Thank you." She brushed her fingertips across his chest. "My first appointment is tomorrow but we have all day to explore the city."

The morning light streamed in through the long windows reflected in his eyes and made them shine. "I'd go to the end of the earth with you, baby," he whispered, and captured her lips, binding her to him once again.

They spent the early part of the morning strolling along the streets near Fifth Avenue, then went across town to the West Village to shop for clothes for Raymond, since it was clear that his stay was going to be much longer than he'd anticipated. They took a cab over to Amsterdam Avenue to Land Thai Kitchen, a place that Ray remembered from one of his trips to New York. He put in a call to Matt, who joined them for a late lunch, and Matt was happy to see that all was apparently back to normal.

Jacqueline was tiring but she didn't want to say anything to Ray. She followed the banter between the two men and realized how happy—almost giddy—she felt inside, like someone was tickling her and she couldn't make them stop. She wasn't going to do anything to jeopardize these emotions of simple happiness. She wanted "normal" for as long as possible. But what she was beginning to realize was that her good days were getting shorter and shorter in length. She wouldn't focus on that. She couldn't.

She reached across the table and covered Raymond's hand with hers. Her smile radiated the love and thanks that she felt for him and the spark in his eyes reflected it right back. *That* was what she'd been so afraid of losing. A moment of fear tightened her chest. She would beat this illness. She had to. She wanted to spend the rest of her life with this man in whatever part of the world that they wound up.

Raymond and Jacqueline waved goodbye to Matt as he hurried toward the subway to make a late afternoon appointment.

"I know I promised myself and you, but…how are you feeling?" he asked as he wrapped one arm around her waist and the other he extended to hail a cab.

To be honest she was thankful that his arm was around her and that they quickly caught a cab. "I'm good," she said, looking up at him with a bright smile. The undertow of fatigue was sucking her out to sea. She allowed him to help her into the cab and she settled in and rested her head on his shoulder. She felt as if none of the pieces of her body were connected or had any substance. As exhausted as she was on some days, she was often terrified of going to sleep for fear of being too exhausted to wake back up.

Raymond pulled her close as the cab sped along Amsterdam Avenue. "I was thinking, baby…"

"Uh-oh," she teased.

"Not funny. I was thinking I would find my way around in your massive kitchen and fix us a great dinner. The fridge and cabinets are stocked. There has to be something in there that I can whip up for us. We can curl up in that big bed and watch a movie. How's that sound?"

She could have cried she was so relieved. "Perfect."

"And I don't want you doing anything. I got this."

"You won't get an argument from me." She snuggled closer and the next thing she knew, Ray was gently nudging her awake.

"We're back and you're going right up to bed. And don't give me any crap about how you're not tired."

She blinked the world back into focus and straightened up. "Fine." She opened the door and stepped out in the cooling afternoon. The breeze somewhat revived her.

Raymond came around from his side of the cab and

walked with her upstairs. Jacqueline Lawson would never simply give in. He didn't give a damn what she said, she wasn't "good." And that terrified him.

Chapter 19

Jacqueline tried her best to put on a good face once they'd gotten inside. Her legs ached and they felt like wet noodles at the same time. All she wanted to do was crawl into bed, but she didn't want to let Ray have any idea how weak and tired she was. She knew the moment that she did, he would hover over her. And that would make her crazy.

"Go on up and relax or nap or whatever you want to do. I'm going to see what we have to fix and plan out something special."

She looped her arms around his waist. "You sure you don't want any help?"

"None." He clasped her shoulders and turned her body toward the stairs. "Go. I'll be up soon."

She stifled a yawn behind feigned wide-eyed indignation. "There's a deep freezer, too," she said, heading for the stairs. "Gotta be something good in there."

"I'll check. Now, go."

She finger-waved goodbye and went upstairs. By the time she reached her bedroom she barely had enough energy to get out of her clothing. She tossed her outfit on the club chair, kicked off her shoes and crawled under the covers. Within moments she was in a deep, dreamless sleep.

Raymond turned on the sound system and adjusted the radio dial to 88.3 WBGO, the jazz station. Soon the unmistakable sound of Sonny Rollins filled the air. Ray bobbed his head and riffed along as he searched through the freezer and found a whole red snapper. He took it out and set it in a pan of water to defrost. He opened the fridge, hoping to find a beer, and much to his surprise there were a half dozen bottles of Carlsberg. As he took one off the shelf, it hit him that whether Jacqueline had intended to or not, he was on her mind when she planned to come to New York. He found an opener, poured the icy brew into a glass and took a long, satisfied swallow. A slow smile moved across his mouth. Jacqueline Lawson was nowhere near as disconnected as she pretended to be. And he knew in his soul that once she really let go, she'd realize that she needed him as much as he needed her.

The sultry sounds of Gloria Lynn's *April in Paris*

was up next on the radio lineup as he washed vegetables and checked for what brand of pasta was handy.

While he was chopping some peppers he heard a cell phone ringing but it wasn't his. He looked around. The ringing was coming from Jacqueline's purse. He walked over to the table. The phone was protruding from the side flap. He picked it up, saw the name and answered.

"Hey, Traci, it's Ray."

"Ray, hi. Um, did I call you by mistake?"

He chuckled. "Naw. This is J's phone. She's asleep. She left her phone downstairs."

"How is she?"

"She says she's fine." He took a swallow of beer and set it down. "But I can see the tightness around her eyes. And she tires easily even if she won't admit it. I can see it." He sat down on the stool at the island counter.

"When is she going to see the specialists?"

"Tomorrow. I'm going with her."

"Good. At least that's some progress. Listen, Ray, Jacqueline is my best friend in the world. She's like a sister to me. I've never betrayed her trust in all the years that we've known each other. But this time I truly believed that what she was doing was wrong. A part of her always knew that. But she was too damned stubborn to admit it."

"I know. I'm glad you told me and I'm pretty sure she is, too. No one really wants to go through any kind of health crisis alone."

"Have you two decided about coming back to L.A.?"

"We haven't gotten that far yet." He paused, looked around. "You should see this place, Traci. She really had every intention of setting up here for the long haul." His fingers reflexively curled into fists as the lingering twinge of hurt snuck up on him.

"She is extremely focused when she puts her mind to it. I told her it was crazy, but she wouldn't listen. I'll probably plan a trip out there as soon as she knows how long the treatments will last. Anyway, tell her that I called and I'll try her tomorrow evening."

"Sure thing."

"And Ray…"

"Yeah…"

"Thanks for not giving up on her."

"I couldn't even if I tried."

"Take care."

"You, too." He got up and returned the phone to Jacqueline's purse.

At some point he was going to have to make some decisions of his own. He had a house in L.A. He couldn't up and leave it. The work was no problem. He was fortunate that he was in the kind of profession where he could work from anywhere in the world. When things settled down he and Jacquie were going to have to do some serious talking about what their lives were going to be like. As much as he loved the vibe of New York City, he was not feeling the cold weather of the North. He'd had enough of that growing up in New Jersey.

One step at a time. The first hurdle was getting Jacqueline through these clinical trials and getting better. After that all the other steps would fall into place. But one of those steps needed to be taken tonight. He'd waited long enough.

When Jacqueline awoke several hours later the sun had already set. The sky above the high-rises was a deep orange. She stretched like a lazy cat and sucked in the mouthwatering aroma of whatever Ray was cooking up in the kitchen.

She slowly sat up. Her head wasn't spinning, and she actually felt as if she had bones in her body and not spaghetti. She swung her feet to the floor and stood, then padded off to the bathroom for a quick shower. When she was done she made swift work of lotioning her body and finding something easy and relaxing to wear. She picked out a salmon-colored satin lounging set that she'd picked up from a Victoria's Secret when she'd been in England. She'd never had a chance to wear it.

She peered into the mirror and applied a light coat of mascara and a splash of tinted lip gloss. She pulled her hair up on top her head and fastened it loosely with a clip. A spritz of her favorite scent went behind her ears, the base of her throat and at her ankles and she was ready to meet her man. She grinned. She liked the thought of that.

Ray didn't hear her approach. Thelonious Monk's "Blue Monk" was keeping him company. He was busy bobbing his head to the music of the great pianist and composer while checking on the progress of his stuffed red snapper. It was a recipe he'd picked up from his mother, but rarely had the chance to use it.

Jacqueline stood in the archway watching him move easily between the stove, the fridge and the sink, turning, prepping and seasoning with ease and periodically miming playing the piano. A half-finished bottle of Carlsberg beer sat on the counter. He'd set out dishes and wineglasses and somehow had located her linen napkins.

He finally sensed her presence and slowly turned toward her with a wide grin on his face. "How long have you been standing there?"

Her arms were folded beneath her breasts. A sparkle was in her eyes. "Long enough catch your piano playing impersonation."

He patted his chest with both hands. "I got skills, girl."

"Yeah, baby," she said with a playful tone of sarcasm tickling her voice. She stepped fully into the kitchen. "Sure smells good." She tried to peek at the pots but he shooed her away.

"Go sit. You're messing up my rhythm."

She ran her hand down the curve of his back and looked up at him from beneath long lashes. Her voice dropped an octave. "I doubt that your rhythm could get messed up."

"Careful," he said, pulling her close. "It's already hot

in the kitchen." He kissed her briefly on the lips and playfully squeezed her bottom. "Want a glass of wine?"

She giggled and swatted his hand away. "Sure." She pulled up a stool and sat at the island.

Raymond took a bottle of white wine from the mini wine fridge beneath the island counter, popped the cork and poured it into her glass.

"Thanks." She took a cooling sip.

He opened the oven and took out the glass tray with the stuffed snapper. The air filled with the tantalizing aroma of cooked spices. He set the steaming tray on the counter, right under Jacqueline's nose.

Her eyes momentarily rolled to the heavens. "Humph, humph, humph, I'm going to have to walk away and take these naps more often if this is what's going to be the result."

"Anytime, baby." He finished off his beer. "Ready to eat or do you want to wait awhile?"

"You really think I can sit here with this in front of me," she said, indicating the golden-brown fish, "and not want to eat?"

Raymond grinned, making his eyes crease in the corners. "Well, in that case..." He arranged the dishes and flatware on the island countertop, cut into the stuffed snapper and placed a hefty chunk on Jacqueline's plate.

The snapper was stuffed with seasoned yellow rice and black beans, scallions, bell peppers and baby shrimp. He took a large glass bowl from the fridge and forked out a finely chopped and colorfully adorned spinach salad onto her plate.

"Nothing like a man who can cook," Jacqueline said in admiration as she looked over her fare.

Raymond loaded up his own plate, placed the tray with the balance of the fish on the top of the stove and then sat opposite her.

Jacqueline poured some wine into his glass. She raised her glass toward him.

"Here's to the chef," she said.

He touched his glass to hers. "To going down easy."

Jacqueline cut into her food and took a mouthful. Her eyes closed in ecstasy. The array of flavors burst in her mouth like a symphony reaching its crescendo.

"Oh, my goodness. This is…"

His brows rose as he waited for the verdict.

"Incredible." She chewed slowly, savoring every morsel. "I don't think I've ever asked you where you learned how to cook like this."

"As quiet as it's kept, I went to Culinary School in New York for about a year."

Her eyes widened. "What? I had no idea."

He grinned. "It was my grandmother that gave me the cooking bug." He forked food into his mouth and chewed thoughtfully. "My folks didn't have money for camp and vacations, so they'd send us off to relatives for the summer. I usually got Grandma Mae. When I would visit with her during the summer she always had me helping out in the kitchen…and the fields…

and the barn." He shook his head and chuckled at the fond memories.

"Where did your grandmother live?"

"Mississippi."

The simple word gave them both a momentary pause. The often dark and tumultuous history of the state was embedded in the memory of African Americans for generations.

"While she had me out in the fields pulling up collard greens, potatoes and snap peas, gathering peaches and apples, she'd tell me what it was like growing up as a young girl in Mississippi. My great-grandparents were both slaves on a small plantation not far from where my grandmother's wood-framed house stood. They instilled in her a sense of pride and dignity and enough good sense not to let it show and get lynched or worse."

He took a long swallow of his wine then refilled both of their glasses. "She told me how she and her brother had barely survived the great flood of '27 when they got separated from their parents. They clung to a tire that they'd hung in a tree for four days."

"Wow, that's amazing."

He gazed off into the distance. "I remember Grandma calling me from playing to sit at that old wobbly wood table in the kitchen and peel peaches for cobbler. It was the kind of hot that sucked the air from your lungs and coated your skin. Too hot for shirts or shoes. Everything stuck to you like fly paper. No air-conditioning, either, back then." He chuckled and shook his head at the memory. "I swear...the heat.... Anyway, Grandma Mae was busy slicing peaches and telling me about how terrified black folks were when those three civil rights workers turned up dead and just a year after Medgar Evers was assassinated. She said, folks wouldn't go out after dark and always walked in twos and threes. Didn't matter what the laws of the land were. It was different in Mississippi."

He pushed his food around with his fork then took a mouthful. "Every time I was at her side for more than a minute, she'd start telling me some story or the other. Like how she used to work for this one white family and she would always cook too much food so that she could take it home for her family. Either they never caught on or didn't care, because she worked for that same family for nearly thirty years."

Jacqueline laughed at the image and tried to imagine this big strapping man as a little boy chopping collards and peeling peaches while he listened to the wisdom of his grandmother, and realized with a pang just how different their lives were growing up.

"She was an amazing woman," he continued thoughtfully. "She'd never gone beyond the third grade but she could read and write, and knew when she was being cheated at the cash register. She could drink a grown man under the table then get up for church on Sunday morning and cook every meal like it was her last."

"It sounds like she's who you got your thirst for storytelling from as well as a love for cooking."

He nodded his head in agreement. "I'd have to agree with you on that one. Of course, I never appreciated it until I was much older."

"Do we ever appreciate what adults have to say when we're kids, especially if we'd rather be doing something else other than listen to them?"

They both chuckled at that one then grew thoughtfully quiet. The silence was as soothing and appropriate as the sounds of Cassandra Wilson singing her rendition of "Time After Time" as if the music was synced up with their emotions.

Raymond looked across the counter at Jacqueline. The aura of serenity that settled around her only illuminated her inner beauty. It was enough to steal his breath away. He didn't want to miss any of these moments. He wanted to be there for her, to catch her when she fell, wait for her to come through the door at night.

"J…"

Her gaze flickered toward him, and a soft smile moved gently across her mouth.

He drew in a short breath and reached into his pants pocket then slowly raised his hand. He opened his palm and the diamond ring that he'd been carrying around like a talisman for months gleamed in his hand. His throat went bone dry and when he began to speak his voice hitched.

Jacqueline's lips parted. Her eyes widened and jumped back and forth from Raymond's face to the future that rested in his hand.

Raymond ran his tongue along his lips, cleared his throat and reached across the table with his free hand to capture Jacqueline's fluttering fingers.

"J. I had a whole speech planned..." The corner of his mouth lifted into a half grin.

Jacqueline blinked rapidly to keep the threatening tears at bay. She tugged on her bottom lip with her teeth.

"Baby...I don't want to be without you. Simple. As many times as I've been around the world the only place I ever wanted to come back to was to you." His brows drew together. "And whatever the future has in store I want us to do it together." He glanced down for a moment then directly at her. "I need you to say yes, J. Marry me."

That did it. She couldn't hold them back any longer. Hot tears of happiness slid down her cheeks and clouded her vision. She wanted to say something, but dammit, her throat was in a knot. All she could do was nod her head like one of those dolls that you set on your dashboard.

Raymond's relief was palpable. He took her shaky hand and slid the ring on her finger. She jumped up from her seat and came around to his side. He pulled her to him and felt her heart hammering in her chest.

"That was scarier than when we were ducking enemy fire in Baghdad," he said into the softness of her hair.

She giggled as the flutter of nerves and adrenaline rippled through her veins. She held her hand out beyond his shoulder to stare at the sparkling beauty.

"It's gorgeous," she murmured in awe.

"Nothing less than what you deserve." He pulled back a bit to look down into her upturned face. "I love you, you know."

Her face heated as her lashes fanned rapidly over her eyes. "I know." She raised her mouth to meet his and the incendiary contact between them took them both by surprise.

Raymond lifted her up into his arms, cleaving her to him, his mouth capturing hers.

Their kiss escalated from heated to explosive. Jacqueline's soft moan of acquiescence seeped into Raymond's blood and fired it. His hands roamed the curves of her body, sliding along the soft fabric then beneath, eager to touch her.

Her body trembled with desire. She caressed his face, ran her fingers along the hard lines of his body, felt the rise of his need for her press urgently against her belly. She desperately wanted him. She wanted him to confirm her existence, to confirm to him the joy that he brought to her life, the hope that he had given her and the courage to battle whatever came their way.

"I love you," she cried. "I do."

He leaned his head back to be able to look into her eyes. "And I want you. Right now. Right here."

Her heart jumped.

He began unbuttoning her top, eased it off her shoulders and tossed it aside. He savored the lush appeal of her round, firm breasts. Tenderly, he ran his thumb across one nipple and then the other, making them rise and harden. Her head dipped back, inviting him to taste her exposed neck. He did then worked his way down to the ripe fruit that he longed for.

Raymond held her securely around the waist while he feasted. With his appetite for her moderately satisfied he continued on his downward exploration, relieving her of her lounging pants that pooled softly at her feet. His thumbs pressed into the soft spaces of her pelvis while his long fingers held her hips firmly still.

When his wet tongue flicked across the exposed bud of her clit her knees buckled. She gripped his shoulders to keep from crumbling into a heap. His mouth and tongue worked in concert, sucking, licking, stroking and building a rhythm that strummed through every inch of her body.

Jolt after jolt of electricity flowed through her. Her moans and whimpers rose in volume and frequency as her climax built like a storm cloud, brewing, dangerous and impending. Her inner thighs trembled. Her heart was beating so fast she could barely catch her breath. An unbearable heat ignited. She was so close. Lights danced behind her closed lids. She wound her hips against the onslaught of his mouth, digging her fingers deeper into his flesh.

And then he lifted her off her feet, and her back was pressed against the cool surface of the double-wide stainless-steel fridge.

Raymond's large hands cupped her behind. She

wrapped her legs around his waist and her arms around his neck.

The force of his entry rammed all the air out her lungs in a gush.

"Ahhhhh," she cried, the rock-hard feel of him filling her in unimaginable ways. She bit down on her lip to keep from screaming but it didn't help. It was too much, too wild, too good.

Raymond buried his face in her neck and then took her mouth again. Every thrust was long, hard and deep, reaching the farthest recesses of her body. Every move he made declared his love for her, his need for her. Confirmed for her that she was the only woman who could make him feel this way.

She knew she couldn't last much longer as the ecstasy built at a blinding speed. Her knees tightened along the cords of his back. His tongue locked with hers and he drove into the hot lava that poured over him and exploded in a gush when her insides convulsed around him, spiraling them both over the edge into utter bliss.

The sounds of her escalated breathing and soft moans played beneath the Stylistics' "You Are Everything."

Jacqueline's head dropped to Raymond's shoulder. She shuddered in his arms. Holding her tight, he slowly backed up and sat down on the stool, taking her with him so that she sat on his lap.

They held each other until their breathing slowly returned to normal.

Raymond tenderly kissed her puffy lips and brushed her hair away from her face. "You okay?"

"Very," she managed. She looked into the light that danced in his eyes. "I think that will be our theme song."

Raymond grinned as the lyrics of love wound to an end. *You are everything...everything is you.*

"Absolutely," he said and sealed that promise with a kiss.

Chapter 20

Raymond held tight to Jacqueline's hand as they approached the doors of the hospital.

Jacqueline stole a quick glance up at him as she stepped to the revolving door.

"It's going to be fine."

She pressed her lips tightly together and nodded her head then pushed through the doors. Once inside the lobby she checked the card in her hand and approached the information console.

"Hi. I'm looking for Dr. Hutchinson. Area D?"

The woman behind the desk asked her to sign in and then gave her directions to the fourth floor.

They squeezed into the elevator with several others and rode to the fourth floor in silence.

The elevator doors swished open. Jacqueline stepped out first. Raymond was right behind her. She looked at the directional information on the wall. They turned left and walked down a long corridor, passing busy nurses and patients being wheeled into exam rooms.

She stopped in front of 4802. She turned to Raymond and was rewarded with a smile of encouragement. She opened the door.

"Hello. Can I help you?"

Jacqueline stepped up to the desk. "Jacqueline Lawson. I have an appointment to see Dr. Hutchinson." Her fingertips gripped the edge of the desk.

The receptionist checked her computer screen then looked up at Jacqueline. "You have one person ahead of you. The wait shouldn't be too long." She reached for a stack of forms and handed them to her. "If you would fill these out while you're waiting."

"Sure." Jacqueline took the forms, a pen and the clipboard and went to sit on one of the waiting-room chairs.

Raymond sat opposite her and took in the surroundings. The colors were soothing. A soft sea-green. There were pictures on the wall of smiling patients. Silk flowers filled several vases. There were two other couples seated on the other side of the room watching a television that was mounted to the wall. A young woman held a sleeping child on her lap. Soothing, elevator-type music played softly in the background.

A woman, accompanied by a doctor, stepped out of

one of the offices. She was smiling. Raymond wanted Jacqueline to come out smiling, as well.

The woman stopped at the desk, spoke briefly to the receptionist and walked out. A nurse stepped out from another room and called the woman with the child.

An eternity seemed to pass by, but it was only about twenty minutes when the receptionist called Jacqueline.

"You can go down the hall to room seven," she said with a pleasant smile on her face.

"Thank you," Jacqueline murmured. She turned to Raymond.

He stood. "You want me in there with you?"

"No." She shook her head and forced a smile. "I'll be fine." She drew in a breath and started toward room seven.

At first Raymond sat. He flipped through every magazine on the table. He got up and paced. He checked his watch. He sat down and crossed and uncrossed his legs. He rested his arms on his thighs and buried his face in his hands. He got up and went to the counter where there was a carafe of water and a coffeemaker. He filled a cup with water and tossed it down in one gulp. He checked his watch. It had been an hour. He returned to his seat and started the process all over again.

Another forty minutes later the door at the end of the corridor opened and Jacqueline stepped out. She turned over her shoulder and said something to the doctor then headed toward the reception area.

Raymond couldn't read the expression on her face. He stood as she drew closer. She stopped at the desk. The receptionist jotted something down on a card and handed it to her. Jacqueline stuck it in her purse then turned and faced Raymond.

"Ready" she said, her throat tight.

He touched her arm. "J?"

"We'll talk outside."

Raymond put his arm around her waist as they walked out. He kept stealing glances at her while they rode down the elevator then outside to the parking lot where they'd left the rented Ford. But she only looked straight ahead.

He opened the passenger-side door, and she got in without a word. He rounded the car, got in and fastened his seat belt.

"J," he said softly. He reached for her hands that she had knotted on her lap.

"Let's go back to the house," she said in a monotone. She turned her head to stare out the window.

Raymond pushed out a breath of frustration and put the car in gear.

Before he could shut the car off, Jacqueline got out and hurried into the house. By the time he got inside she'd gone upstairs. He found her sitting in the window seat.

He gathered himself, prepared for whatever she would tell him. He could handle it. But she was not going to shut him out. Not again. Not this time. He crossed the room and sat next to her.

"Talk to me. Tell me what the doctor said."

She glanced away. She folded her arms beneath her breasts.

"I…he said that based on my tests…" Her voice hitched. "He said that based on the results sent to him from L.A., he didn't believe that the trials would help. The results from the treatment…would take…too long." Her chest heaved and she pressed her fist to her mouth. A tear spilled down her cheek.

Raymond's mind screeched to a halt. Time seemed to stand still. His nostrils flared as he sucked in air. He pulled her to him and held her against his chest. Her sobs rocked her body.

"Maybe he's wrong," he said, grabbing for straws. "They have to test you again. At least try!"

She shook her head and pulled away from him. She moved away to the other side of the room and sat on the edge of the bed.

"It was five years ago," she began in a faraway voice. "I was on assignment. A chemical explosion." She swallowed. "I was there to take pictures of the site. There was a smell. Weeks later. There was still a smell. But they swore it was safe." Her brows drew together as the memory formed. "I went into the buildings with some of the investigators. We had on masks. It was so hot. I…was working on some shots but it was hard to see with the mask. Stupidly, I took my mask off. For the shot." She snorted in disgust. "I remember stepping over some rubble. The floor was slick. I bent down to get a shot of a single shoe. The only thing left…of someone."

Raymond remembered that assignment. He remembered the photograph. It was set against twisted metal and concrete, a stark reminder of the utter devastation. That photograph won her an award.

"It was probably two years later that I started not feeling like myself. No one could figure out what was wrong. I went from one doctor to the other. Eventually, I got used to it. Then about a year ago they finally diagnosed aplastic anemia, a result of over exposure to toxic chemicals." She drew in a breath. "The doctors tried all of the treatments available. But about six months ago… they stopped having any benefit. My doctor recommended the new clinical trials." She looked at Raymond and threw her hands up in resignation. "So here I am."

"You went back home to Baton Rouge to say goodbye, didn't you?" The realization of it all hit him in the gut.

She couldn't meet his steady gaze.

"J…"

"Yes! I knew if the treatment didn't work…I…" Her shoulders shook.

Raymond gathered her close. "There has to be something that they can do."

She shook her head against his chest. "Bone marrow transplant is the only other option. I've been on the list for months."

He knew what she was holding back. "Ask your brother."

"No." She pulled away. "I won't." She looked him square in the eye. "I won't. I can't." With that, she stormed off into the bathroom and slammed the door behind her.

Raymond stood in the center of the room. The enormity of what Jacqueline had revealed weakened him to his soul. He wouldn't lose her. The trials, new medication, something had to work. And if getting the bone marrow transplant from her brother was the only way to save her then he didn't give a damn what she thought she wanted. He was just as stubborn as she was.

He snatched up his cell phone and went downstairs.

Chapter 21

Rafe disconnected the call. Slowly, he set his phone down on the nightstand. The woman in his bed stirred. He glanced at her over his shoulder. He picked up his boxers from the floor and put them on then walked out into the front room. He went to the bar and poured himself a glass of bourbon.

He walked to the window. The sun was setting over Louisiana. Tomorrow he would be on a plane to Washington. He tossed back the last of his drink. But tonight he had a beautiful woman in his bed and he intended to make the most of it. He put the glass down and returned to his bedroom.

Branford strode down the halls of the Senate building. Frustration rimmed his eyes. Another fruitless two hours of debating over the points of the health care bill. If certain senators had their way, they would overturn the bill and set the country back decades. It was unconscionable that anyone with an ounce of humanity in them could sleep at night knowing that they were responsible for denying poor people, women and children the health care that they deserved.

"Of course there are things wrong with the bill," he said to Claude, his Chief of Staff. "But for Godsake, is the answer to overturn it?"

"None of this has anything to do with the bill."

Branford grumbled under his breath. "We all know that," he said, his disgust evident. "If one of them would have had the balls to come up with it, there wouldn't be a problem."

Deep in conversation, they breezed by Branford's secretary and walked into his office. Branford stopped at the door.

Rafe turned from the window overlooking the epicenter of the country to face his father. He adjusted his tie. "Dad. Claude." He tipped his head in greeting. "Melissa said I could wait for you here. I told her not to say anything. I hope you don't mind." He ran his hand along the smooth surface of the enormous oak desk.

"I'll be in my office," Claude said. "Rafe, good to see you."

"You, too."

Branford stepped into the room and shut the door behind him. He walked over to the wet bar and poured a half tumbler of bourbon. "What are you doing here, Rafe? Are you in some kind of trouble again?"

Rafe snorted a laugh. "Can't a son come to see his old man at his place of business?"

Branford crossed to his desk, picked up a sterling silver letter opener then set it back down. "Nothing you do is ever that simple." He looked hard at his son and took a long swallow of his drink. He moved in deliberate paces to the conversation grouping of seating.

Rafe came to stand on the opposite side of his father's desk. "We need to talk."

"I'm listening." He sat down in the chocolate-brown leather club chair. He rested his right ankle on his left knee.

"It's about Aunt Jacquie."

Branford's expression tightened. He glanced away. "What about her?"

"She's sick. Really sick, and she won't make it unless you help her."

Branford's gaze locked with Rafe's. He pushed up from his seat.

"No. I think you need to sit down."

Rafe lowered himself into an identical club chair. He rested his forearms on his thighs and leaned forward.

Rafe had seen his father in many circumstances. He'd always been impenetrable, stoic and almost distant. The closest he'd come to displaying any real noticeable emotion was when Louisa, his wife and mother of his children, died. Then the veneer had cracked. Then and now.

Branford's fingers clenched and unclenched. His always straight-back was bowed.

"Does she hate me that much that she wouldn't tell me that she…needed me?" He looked up at his son and water rimmed his eyes.

Rafe's stomach clenched as the depth of his father's pain became his own. "She gets her stubborn streak honestly."

Branford's eye flickered to his son. A flash of admiration was there for an instant. He pushed himself to his feet. He went to his desk and pressed the intercom. "Melissa, I need you to get me on the next shuttle flight to New York." He glanced at Rafe. "And a seat for my son."

Jacqueline had taken her camera and quietly left the house right after sunup. She'd lain awake most of the night. Her thoughts twisted and turned on an endless journey. She'd put so much faith into the possibility of being a good candidate for the medical trials that she'd allowed herself to dream again. She'd foolishly let down her guard, opened her heart fully and let Raymond all the way in. She'd embraced his words of love and gave him hers. She'd taken down the wall of protection and now her spirit, the thing that propelled her through life, was shattered. And as much as Raymond professed his life and his vow to stand by her side, it would change nothing.

The city was wrestling itself awake. The towering gray buildings that pierced the muted sky made for dynamic images. The lighting, as always, was key.

She walked along Seventy-Second Street, stopped and snapped a shot of an old white-haired couple walking gingerly hand in hand down the street. The husband leaned closer and said something to his wife that caused her head to roll back and girlish laughter to spark from her throat. In that instant the years peeled away and they were young lovers. Jacqueline captured them as they had once been, but more important that "once had been" moment never changed for them. They would always be those young lovers in each other's eyes.

Jacqueline's vision clouded. She blinked away the future that she would never see. She would never walk down this avenue or any other with Raymond five, ten, twenty years from now. They would never have that moment that she'd shot.

Raymond deserved a chance at what she'd just witnessed. His life shouldn't be spent watching her wither away and being strong for her. He deserved a life and a family.

When she looked across the street the couple was gone as if they had never been there. Or perhaps only there long enough for her to know what she needed to do. She kept walking.

* * *

Raymond refused to get himself worked up. It was close to one in the afternoon and Jacqueline had yet to return.

He'd heard her moving stealthily around the room, opening and closing drawers, tiptoeing in and out of the bathroom, then collecting her camera equipment from the closet.

Jacqueline used her art as a balm. Whenever she needed to work through a problem or vent she rose with the sun and went in search of the perfect shot, finding the answers to whatever was eating at her.

He knew that she was looking for answers this morning. So he'd remained still, feigning sleep, not interfering with her process. After she'd stormed off earlier the prior day, she'd emphatically refused to discuss anything else related to her health. It was done as far as she was concerned. And as she always had done in the face of adversity she went inside herself. It was a trait that he both admired and resented. If only she would truly allow him to carry part of the burden. But she refused.

His call to Rafe had been an act of desperation. Jacqueline would be furious but he was willing to deal with her wrath. He only hoped that his gamble would pay off.

He heard the front door open and then close. He put down his coffee cup on the counter. Jacqueline walked in and his felt more unsettled than he'd ever felt in his life.

She put her camera bag down on the table. "Hi," she said softly.

"Hi."

"I didn't want to wake you."

He simply looked at her, waiting for her to tell him what it was she'd discovered.

She crossed the space and sat down at the island counter. "Any more coffee?"

"Sure." He took a mug from the cabinet and poured her a cup.

"Thanks." She added a teaspoon of sugar and plenty of cream.

He smiled to himself. Jacqueline always wanted coffee in her cream instead of the other way around. "Beautiful day out," he said to take up the space that seemed to grow in leaps and bounds between them.

"I'd forgotten how tranquil this city could be in the early hours."

He studied the contemplative expression on her face as the nerves in his belly grew tighter and tighter. "Maybe we can do something later. Take in a movie or a show somewhere. There's always something going on in New York."

"Maybe," she said noncommittally and took a sip of her coffee. "You always did make good coffee," she said, offering up a half smile.

The banal banter was like a conversation between two strangers. And the long silences in between the attempts at normalcy was deafening.

Raymond took his mug to the sink then turned to Jacqueline and his heart stood still.

Jacqueline was taking off her ring. Gently she placed it on the counter. "I saw a couple today," she began. Her gaze rose to meet his. "They were about eighty and very much in love." Her throat worked up and down. "And…I realized in that moment when I snapped their picture, captured that moment of joy that their moment could never be our moment." Her bottom lip trembled ever so slightly.

Raymond didn't move.

"You should go back to L.A. You deserve more than what the rest of whatever life I have can offer you."

His jaw clenched. "Is that really what you want, J, to spend the rest of your life alone? Doesn't the fact that I love you more than anything in this world mean anything to you?"

It wasn't what she wanted, but it was the way it had to be. You don't burden the people that you love. You didn't do that. She couldn't do that, not to Ray.

She pushed the ring toward him. "Go home, Ray." She got up from her seat turned and walked out of the room.

Jacqueline didn't know what she'd expected Ray to do, yell, demand, plead or come after her. She crossed the bedroom to the window seat. She pushed aside the curtain and stared unseeingly at life unfolding below. She'd made the right decision, hadn't she?

There was a part of her that desperately wanted to spend every waking moment with Ray. Tour the world, explore new things and not waste an instant of their time together. But wouldn't it be worse for him later? Wasn't it best to end it now?

A black SUV with tinted windows pulled onto her street and slowed. She peered a bit closer. The vehicle had government plates. She knew Bill and Hilary had a place in the city but she was pretty sure it wasn't on this street. Probably a local politico.

She started to look away when the car pulled to a stop in front of her house. The driver got out and opened the passenger door. Branford stepped out. Tall, handsome as ever and dapper in his steel-gray suit, snow-white shirt and burgundy tie. His close-cropped salt-and-pepper hair glistened in the afternoon light. Rafe got out behind him, a younger and even more handsome version of his father.

The air stuck in her lungs. She jumped up and backed away from the window. *What in world…* Her skin began to tingle. Maybe it was some bizarre coincidence that they were here of all places. That had to be it.

The doorbell rang. She gasped.

She hurried to the entrance of her bedroom and heard the front door open and the sound of heavy male voices. Drawing in a deep, steadying breath, she went downstairs.

The trio's heads turned when she appeared in the archway of the sitting room.

Raymond strode toward her. He clasped her shoulders with steely fingers.

"How could you—"

He cut her right off. "You're going to listen to what he has to say," he said in a harsh, no-nonsense whisper.

Her chest heaved up and down.

Raymond glanced over his shoulder at Rafe and subtly tilted his head.

Rafe caught the signal. He approached warily, ready and willing to be chastised by his aunt. He bent down to kiss her cheek. "Nice place you have, Aunt J." His mouth flickered into a devilish grin.

She was so furious she couldn't speak. She only glared at him.

"Got any bourbon?" he asked Raymond, clasping him on the shoulder as they walked out, leaving Jacqueline and Branford alone.

Jacqueline stared at her brother. Even now, after all these years, she still felt like the little pain in the ass sister.

"Mind if I sit?"

"When have you ever needed my permission for anything? You've always done what you wanted."

He ignored the barb and took a seat on the couch. "As have you."

She flinched at the stab of truth. "Why are you here, Branford? I know you didn't come from wherever you were to make small talk."

"No, I didn't." He paused a beat. "Please, sit."

She folded her arms, wanting to be obstinate for obstinance's sake, but finally gave in. She sat on the love seat that was arranged opposite to him and watched the array of emotions play across his face as whatever was going through his mind was being relived.

"When Louisa got sick…" he finally said, his voice so reverential that she barely recognized it, "I took her to every doctor, every specialist that money could buy. We tried every treatment available until we'd exhausted all possibilities." He lowered his head and linked his fingers together, and seemed to study the simple gold wedding band that he'd never taken off. He unhurriedly turned it on his finger.

He drew in a long breath and slowly exhaled. "When I met Louisa all those years ago, it was the first time in my life that I had something to live for beyond my own ambition."

Jacqueline was dumbstruck by her brother's confession, his display of vulnerability. It was a side of him that she'd never seen.

"The funny thing is, it was Louisa that was the strong one. She was the one that got me through it. She never lost her joy for life, her unflappable curiosity. And even in those last days she never gave up on living every minute to the fullest and filling every moment surrounded by the people who loved her and that she loved." He focused on his sister. "That is what I treasure most, what still gets me through the days without her."

She'd always wondered why her brother had never

remarried. It wasn't as if he didn't have any number of women who would willingly step into the role of Mrs. Branford Lawson. She'd believed that he was too self-absorbed. Now she knew. He would never love anyone the way that he'd loved Louisa and he was good with that.

"And then David…"

There it was, the elephant in the room.

"I suppose you don't know that I went to see Maurice a few months ago."

Her body stiffened. Her nephew, David's only son, had been estranged from the family for as long as she and for the very same reason. They both believed that Branford was in some way responsible for David's death.

"You…saw Maurice?"

He nodded his head. "And I told him what I should have told him years ago, what I should have told you."

In agonizing detail, he explained to her those days that had been unspoken until recently. David had gotten in way over his head by manipulating investments of his clients. It was all coming to a head. He was being investigated and he'd come to Branford to bail him out. Branford refused. Rather than spend years in prison, David had taken his own life and left a note that Maurice had found, blaming Branford for turning his back on him.

Branford had used all of his powers and called in numerous favors to quiet the investigation and made arrangements to anonymously pay off the clients that David had swindled.

Jacqueline's heart was pounding. The blood was rushing to her head. All this time…all this animosity…the years of anger and loss…

Her gaze slowly rose to meet her brother's, and for the first time in longer than she could remember she actually saw him. Not as this towering, unbending figure, but as a man with a heart and soul that had been broken just as much as hers. But he'd never once lauded what he had done for David in the end. Instead, he took the rebuke and he'd lived with it in stoic silence for years.

"Bran…I…"

He held up his hand. "I'm not telling you all of this to get your sympathy vote." He tried a smile. "I'm telling you because I lost two of the most important people in my life because either there was nothing I could do or I acted too late." He swallowed hard. "I don't want to lose you, too." He voice wavered. "Let me do this for you." He paused. "Please."

Tears slid slowly down her cheeks. She pushed herself to her feet and sat beside him. She looked into his eyes and caressed the rugged jaw. All she could do was nod her head, *yes*.

Relief rushed through Branford in waves as he pulled his sister close against his chest, resting his chin on her head so that she would never see the tears in his eyes.

Chapter 22

"I knew you would never go to him," Raymond was saying as he and Jacqueline lay spooning together in the center of the king-size bed.

"You're right, I wouldn't have." She turned around to face him. "But if you hadn't done what you did, I may have never really known my brother, the man he is beneath all the pomp and circumstance. He's so much more than a public figure."

"Sometimes adversity and trials bring out the best in people. If they're given the chance."

Her gaze moved lovingly across his face. "So I'm learning."

Rafe and Branford had stayed for dinner and Raymond had miraculously convinced them to try one of his imported beers. They were hooked. Then it became a battle of the chefs as Jacqueline was relegated to a seat on the sidelines while the men tried to outdo each other in the kitchen. Her mouth hung open as she watched them slice, dice and marinate. She knew that Raymond had cooking skills but she had no idea that her brother and nephew could throw down, as well.

Branford found all the ingredients for a spicy sausage jambalaya just like their mother used to make. Not to be outdone, Rafe cooked up grilled chicken and shrimp kebabs and Raymond sautéed steak that melted like butter in your mouth. Mounds of yellow rice and three kinds of vegetables rounded out the meal.

After stuffing themselves, they'd sat around in the living room. She sipped wine while the men alternated between bourbon and beer. How Branford and Rafe managed to make it out to their car was inspiring.

Rafe was heading back to Baton Rouge in the morning and Branford made arrangements to meet Jacqueline at the hospital for tests. Both had declined her offer to have them stay at her house. Branford had a standing reservation at the Hilton and got an extra room for Rafe.

"It was a good day," Jacqueline said reflectively.

"I like your family."

She was thoughtful for a moment. A genuine smile of happiness lifted the corners of her mouth. "So do I."

* * *

Jacqueline, Raymond and Branford stood outside of the hospital. Branford's car and driver waited at the curb. It had begun to drizzle.

"The doctor said they should be in touch in a few days with the results of the tests," Branford said, looking into Jacqueline's eyes. He gripped her upper arm. "It'll be a match and I'll be back."

She released a sigh. "Thank you."

"No, thank you." The corner of his mouth rose ever so slightly.

A clap of thunder punctuated the air. He glanced up. "I'd better go. We'll talk." He stuck his hand out to Raymond. "Don't let her push you around too much. Bad habit of us Lawsons."

Raymond chuckled. "So I've been learning." He gripped Branford's hand and gave it a firm shake that said more than any words.

"You two take care of each other." He ducked into the car and it pulled away.

"Come on, it's going to pour any minute," Raymond urged, looping his arm around Jacqueline's waist and ushering her toward the parking lot.

They made it back to the car just as the sky opened up and the deluge came down.

Just darting from the car to the house they were drenched, and they tumbled into the house laughing and shaking off water.

They trooped up to the bedroom and Raymond did the honors of stripping Jacqueline of her wet clothing.

"You are so beautiful," he said, looking at her standing naked before him. He tucked a wet strand of hair behind her ear.

She tugged at the hem of his T-shirt that clung to his broad chest and pulled it up and over his head. She pressed a hot kiss to his exposed flesh. "You're not so bad yourself," she said in a thick voice. She unhooked his belt buckle and unzipped him.

"Still want to banish me to L.A.?" He trailed a finger down the center of her chest all the way to her navel. He felt her stomach flutter.

She tilted her head back a bit. "I think I've reconsidered my hasty decision."

"I see." His fingers flexed across her downy pubic hair.

"Hmmm." She sighed.

"I think I need to be convinced."

She grinned and her eyes darkened. She hooked her fingers into his belt loops and backed up toward the bed pulling him with her. She plopped down on the bed, and pulled him between her legs. She glanced up at him from beneath the fan of her lashes before tugging his pants and boxers down over his hips and legs.

He was ready for her before she touched him. Her soft fingers wrapped around his stiff length and brought the tip to her waiting mouth.

Rain pounded against the window. The heavens rumbled and the sky lit up like daytime.

All they heard and saw was each other.

The waiting was hardest. Each time her phone rang she prayed that it was the hospital calling with news. A week had gone by. They'd said it would be a few days. Her anxiety grew.

She was coming out of the shower when Raymond handed her the phone. "It's the hospital."

Her mouth tightened. No matter what they said she would handle it. "Thanks." She took the phone. "Hello. Yes, this is Jacqueline Lawson." She covered the mouthpiece. "They want me to hold for Dr. Hutchinson." It felt like an eternity before he finally came on the line. "Yes. Are you sure? Of course. Yes. I'll make arrangements. Thank you, Doctor." She hung up the phone on its base.

"Well? What did he say?"

"He said he doesn't usually give information over the phone but he knew how long I'd been waiting."

"What did he say?" Raymond urged.

A smile like daybreak spread across her mouth. "He said Branford is a perfect match and they want to set up the procedure as soon as possible."

Raymond swooped her up into his arms amidst her tears and laughter. He rained kisses all over her face. "Oh, God, J. It's going to be all right. You're going to be all right." He squeezed her to him and buried his face in her hair.

She squeezed her eyes shut as she allowed herself to be enveloped in the love of his embrace. Now, someday in the very distant future, they would be that gray-haired couple that some eager photographer would capture and be inspired by.

Chapter 23

It took Branford a week to reschedule meetings and make arrangements to be out of D.C. The doctor assured him that the procedure wouldn't be that painful. They would remove the marrow from the back of both of his hips. He would be given a local anesthetic and, barring any complications, could leave the hospital the same day. However, he recommended that Branford take some time off to give himself the opportunity to recover from any discomfort from the harvested site.

The one thing he was thankful for as the anesthesiologist put the mask over his face was that this was New York and not Baton Rouge or Washington where he was recognizable. Here he had a semblance of anonymity and his being in the hospital, although under an assumed name, would not turn into a media circus. Contrary to what many believed about him, he was a private person. His grandstanding only came about when politics and business were involved.

He turned his head to see his sister on the table next to him. *This time he would get it right.* It was the last thing he remembered before sleep overtook him.

"They're going to keep her in isolation for two days to make sure that there is no infection and that the procedure worked," Raymond said to Branford as they waited outside of Jacqueline's room while she was being settled in by the nurse.

Branford nodded. He checked his watch. He'd been out of recovery for nearly an hour. The doctor said he could leave as soon as he was ready and had someone to pick him up. He was ready. The longer he stayed the more he thought about the countless days and hours he'd spent with Louisa in hospitals just like this.

"Hey, you okay? How are you feeling?"

Branford blinked him into focus. "Not bad. A little sore." He chuckled. "Tell her…I'll call."

"Don't you want to wait and talk to her yourself?"

He patted Raymond's shoulder. "She has you. Take care of yourself and take care of my sister for me." He turned and walked out.

Raymond's gaze followed Branford until he was swallowed up by the comings and goings of staff, visitors and patients. One of these days he would get the hang of the whole Lawson "thing."

"You can go in now," the nurse said.

"Thanks."

"You'll need to put on a gown and a mask."

He took a sealed package that contained a blue gown, booties for his feet and a mask. He donned his new attire and pushed through the glass door.

Jacqueline's eyes lit up when she saw him. "Well, maybe if you can't make it as a journalist you can do stand-ins for a doctor." Her voice was a little raspy from the anesthetic.

"Very funny." He pulled up a chair and sat next to the bed. He took her hand. "How are you feeling?"

"Pretty good." She squeezed his fingers. "Where's Bran?" She tried to peek around him.

"He left. Said he needed to get back but he would call you."

She frowned. "Oh." She rested her head against the pillows. She shouldn't be surprised but for some reason she was. Branford's behavior, his admissions and his displays of true humanity were such aberrations from the man he presented to the world that he was probably in shock. *Still.*

When Raymond brought Jacqueline back to her New York home she was stunned to find her home filled to near bursting with her nephew Rafe who'd brought along a statuesque model-type named Celeste, Justin, who was looking more like his older brother every day, her nieces Lee Ann, Dominique and Desiree, their husbands Preston Graham, Spence Hampton and the newest nephew in-law Trevor Jackson ensconced in her living room ready to party.

Whoops of delight swirled around her as she was engulfed in hugs and kisses and a barrage of questions that she couldn't begin to answer.

"Oh, my goodness." She pressed her hand to her chest and looked from one loving face to the next. "I can't believe…" She turned to Raymond who had a sly grin on his face. "You knew!"

"Guilty," he said, delighted at the joy that glowed from her eyes.

Her nieces swarmed around her, ushering her inside. The already stunning sitting room was filled with balloons and flowers and cards. Something delicious-smelling filled the air. Soft music played in the background.

Rafe and his sisters began handing out champagne flutes. He gave the bottle of champagne to Raymond. "Do the honors."

Jacqueline looked around at her family, at all the love that was in the room. There was only one thing missing—her brother. Had it not been for him…none of this would be happening.

The cork in the champagne bottle popped to the delight of the group, and Raymond began filling glasses.

The doorbell rang.

"It better not be strippers," Jacqueline said. Every-one broke out in laughter.

Raymond handed the bottle to Rafe. "I'll get it." He went to the door.

Moments later Branford walked in, with his arm around the shoulder of his nephew Maurice. A beauti-ful young woman held Maurice's hand.

A collective gasp and then another flurry of squeals broke out when they saw their cousin Maurice. The only one who didn't seem surprised was Rafe who watched the event unfold with a cool smile.

Maurice took the greetings in stride, doling out kisses and handshakes until he finally made his way to Jacqueline.

"Hey, Aunt J."

Her throat was so tight she could barely say his name. "Maurice." She stroked his cheek to make sure that all of the excitement wasn't playing tricks on her. She grabbed him in a tight hug. "It's so good to see you," she said softly. "So good to see you with your uncle."

He stepped back and smiled down at her. "We were wrong for a long time. But all that has changed now."

She nodded in agreement. "I know. I know."

He turned to the lady on his arm. "Aunt J, this is Layla."

"Nice to meet you, Layla."

"I've heard so much about you, about your whole family. I'm really happy to be here and that you're doing well."

"Thank you. Well, please, come in. I have no idea what all is planned but make yourselves comfortable."

She walked over to where Branford was getting his champagne flute filled. She touched his back. He turned to face her.

"Hey, *cher.*"

He hadn't called her by the endearing term since she was a little girl. Her heart swelled.

"Thank you. Thank you for everything."

He looked embarrassed and cleared his throat. "Mmm-hmm."

Jacqueline grinned. Some things never changed, but that was just fine. She loved her brother just the way he was. She leaned close. "Don't worry, I'll never tell a soul that your heart isn't made out of stone. You secret is safe with me." She kissed his cheek just as Raymond began tapping the side of his glass to get everyone's attention.

By degrees, the room quieted.

Raymond looked around at the expectant faces then settled his gaze on Jacqueline.

"I want to thank each of you for being here today to toast Jacqueline's recovery and celebrate her new lease on life. I especially want to thank Branford." He tilted his glass in Branford's direction. He swallowed and pulled in a deep breath. "Maybe only once in your life you meet someone that makes you realize that the only thing you want to do is spend the rest of your life with them." The couples in the room stole loving glances at each other. "That's what happened to me when I met

Jacquie. I'm not gonna lie. This woman has put me through hell." Smatterings of laughter danced in the air. "I wouldn't have it any other way."

He reached in his pocket and took out the diamond ring. Jacqueline's face flamed. Raymond was moving toward her. "I gave this to her after carrying it around in my pocket for months." He stepped closer. "She took it…but just like a feisty, stubborn Lawson she gave it back. So I figured maybe I did it wrong." He lowered himself to one knee and took her left hand in his. "You're my everything, J."

She couldn't breathe.

"Whatever the world has in store for us we can do it together. Me and you. You're my other half. I'm not whole without you. Marry me, J."

Jacqueline sniffed back her tears and sank down on her knees in front of him. She cupped his face in her hands. "Yes, yes, for real, for always."

Raymond drew her into a kiss that made the rest of the world disappear.

The assemblage erupted into deafening cheers and applause.

Jacqueline was giddy with joyous laughter as Raymond pulled her to her feet and once again placed the diamond on her finger. "I'll never take it off again," she whispered.

He hooked his arm around her waist. "Remember you have witnesses this time," he teased, gazing down into her eyes.

Everyone raised their glasses in a toast to the newly engaged couple.

Jacqueline's nieces swirled around her to get a look at the stunning diamond and then each began swapping stories of their own romantic proposals.

The men congratulated Raymond with hearty slaps on the back and a string of "welcome to the family."

The welcome-home-turned-engagement party lasted past midnight.

By the time everyone left to return to their hotel, Jacqueline was exhausted but still so wired that she couldn't sleep.

"What an incredible day," she whispered into the dimness of their bedroom.

"Yeah, it was. Happy?"

"I'm beyond happy. And to see Maurice…and Bran…"

"They all love you very much."

"I know that now. It was selfish of me to stay away, to let my own misguided judgment keep me away." She turned on her side to face him. "You made it all possible. Everything."

"For you. I did it for you."

"I love you, Raymond Jordan, and I can't wait to be your wife."

"I'm going to hold you to that." He turned her onto her back and slowly made her promise him over and over again.

Epilogue

Eight Months Later—Baton Rouge, LA

Raymond and Jacqueline had been back to the West Coast several times in the past few months, tying up loose ends. They'd decided to consolidate their homes in California. Jacqueline sold her condo and of course never one to "move in with a man," Raymond sold his place as well and they bought a place together in the valley.

Jacqueline loved the house in New York too much to give it up, so they decided to keep it as a second home.

Raymond had been on several short-term assignments overseas in the past few months, but Jacqueline opted to stay close to home and took on a few local gigs. But the travel bug was nipping at her again and she knew it wouldn't be long before she would have her passport stamped.

So much had happened in the past few months but it was years in the making. Hearts had been healed. Impassable roads had been crossed and a future rife with endless possibilities was there for the taking. She had her brother back. She had her family back. And a man who loved her unconditionally.

"Ready?"

Traci stood behind her and adjusted her headpiece. The two sister-friends smiled at each other in the mirror.

"Ready."

The music floated to the rafters, and the gathering rose to their feet on either side of the aisle.

The ushers opened the doors to the sanctuary and a collective ahhh mixed with the music. The form-fitting Vera Wang gown, splashed with hand-sewn jewels and seed pearls with a daring low-cut back that stopped just in time, couldn't have been worn by anyone other than Jacqueline.

"I've done this a few times," Branford said in a teasing whisper. "Just follow my lead." He winked at her.

Jacqueline clasped Branford's bent elbow, looked down the flower-strewn aisle to the man who held her heart, and walked with her brother at her side into what she knew would be an amazing future.

* * * * *

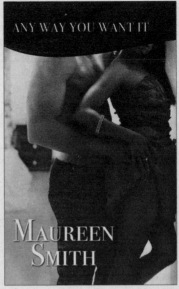

A classic novel in the bestselling Hideaway series!

NATIONAL BESTSELLING AUTHOR

ROCHELLE ALERS

Homecoming

Reporter Dana Nichols has come home to Mississippi determined to uncover the truth behind her parents' long-ago murder-suicide tragedy and finally clear her family name. The last thing she expects is her instant attraction to handsome, dedicated doctor Tyler Cole. As she and Tyler search for answers, they end up walking a dangerous line between trust and uncertainty that will put their future love at stake....

"Homecoming is the latest in Ms. Alers' Hideaway series, and boy, what an intense installment it's proven to be!"
— *RT Book Reviews* on *Homecoming*

Available December 2012 wherever books are sold!

REQUEST YOUR FREE BOOKS!

2 FREE NOVELS
PLUS 2 *FREE GIFTS!*

KIMANI ROMANCE ™

Love's ultimate destination!